ROOMMATES

A DARK SAPPHIC ROMANCE

CASSIE HARGROVE

Copyright © 2022 by A.L. Ryan/Cassie Hargrove

All rights reserved.

No part of this book may be reproduced in any form or by any electronic or mechanical means, including information storage and retrieval systems, without written permission from the author, except for the use of brief quotations in a book review.

Cover Design: Laura Sunday/Genesis Graphics

Proofreading: Kalynn Trammel

PREFACE

This book isn't for the faint of heart.

While there are some scenes that will make you laugh, it also deals with the after effects of rape.

Triggers:
- SA off page
- Graphic T0r+ure and Dea+h on page

Please go into this book with these main triggers in mind. I hope you enjoy it!

- A.L. Ryan/Cassie Hargrove

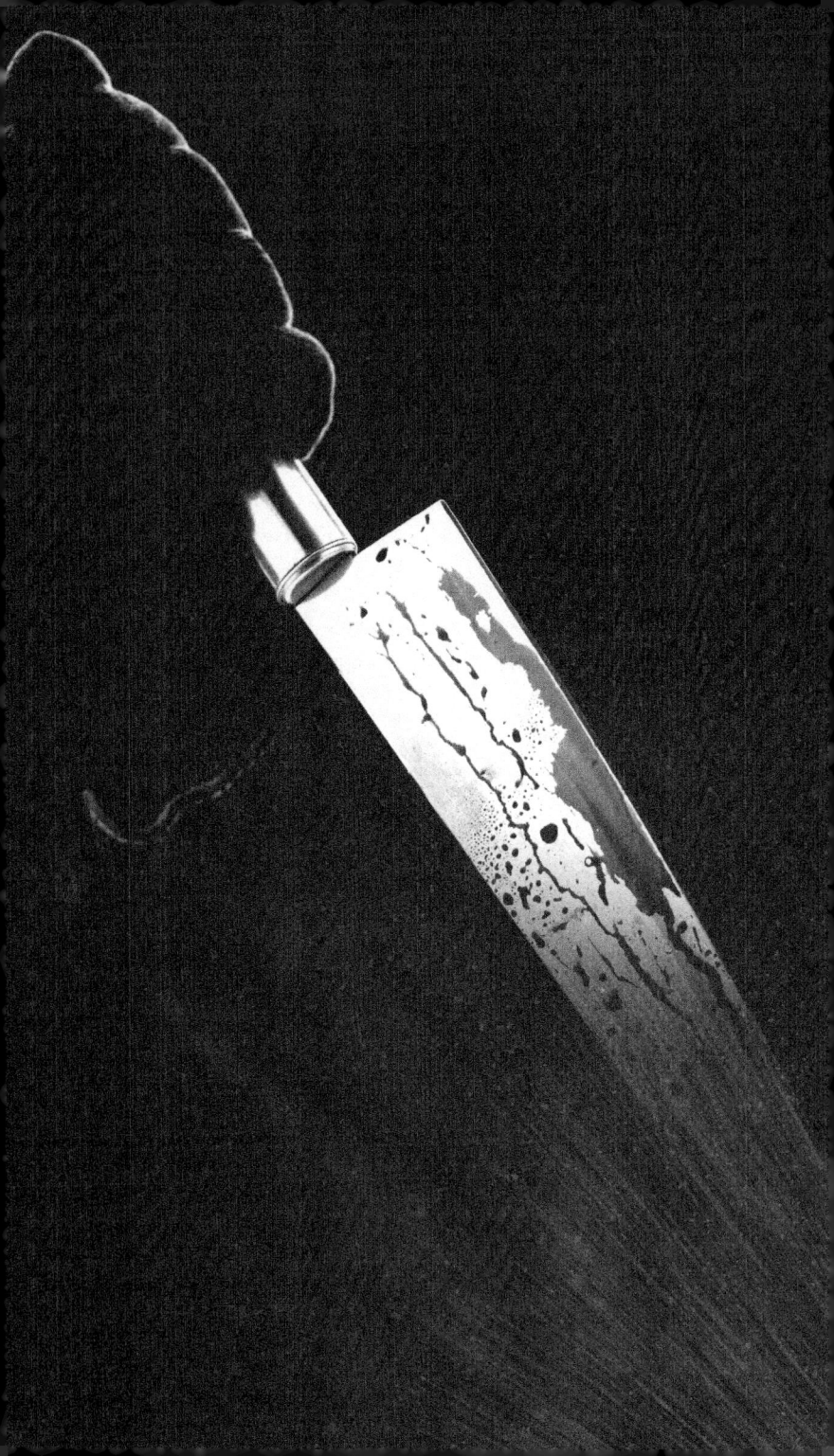

CHAPTER 1
DARIA

THIS IS POINTLESS.

Dad insisting I go to college to experience a 'normal' life makes zero sense. He's always been determined to give me a normal life, but he knows I'm exactly like him, so why try to force this?

He and Mom were never meant to be together. She was just a night of passion while he was on a job. Neither of them expected to get pregnant with me. He didn't even give her his name that night, so the fact that she tracked him down to tell him about the pregnancy impressed the hell out of him.

But my mother is nothing if not tenacious and stubborn. I get that from her, and it drives Dad completely insane. He constantly curses the universe for giving me both of their stubborn attributes because I'm a force to be reckoned with once I decide on something.

"How are you feeling, sweetheart?" Dad asks me.

We're sitting in the back of his black SUV as his driver—and bodyguard—maneuvers us through city traffic.

Carlos has been with my father for as long as I can remember and may be his only friend that knows of my existence. With Dad's career choice, he wants to keep me hidden so his enemies can't use me against him. We don't even share a last name.

Mom likes to tell me how terrified she was when she found out Dad's true identity and how she almost didn't tell him she was pregnant. She didn't want to be a part of that life.

I do.

I understand why she was fearful. Anyone who walks the straight and narrow would be, but this is in my blood. I want to be a killer, just like my father, the great Kane Fitzgerald. Or as others call him; The Hunter.

I want to take over the family business, but apparently I have to get college out of the way first.

"I'm good, Daddy," I say, putting on a fake happy face.

He snorts, shaking his head and reaching over to hold my hand in his own.

"Can't fool me, kid. I know my blood is pumping through those veins of yours, but we have to appease your mother." He gives me a hard look.

They never tried to make things work after she got pregnant. Actually, Dad went so far out of his way to keep me a secret to protect us that whenever I did get to see him, it was at this remote cabin he owns in the mountains. A place no one knows exists. Not even his boss. Well, if you could call him that. Dad is a contract killer. The best in the business, but he has an open-ended contract with one of the mafia families in the DC area to kill people that are too high profile for one of their men to touch.

I'm not exactly sure why he's afraid of them knowing who I am, since they could never kill him. They know it too, but it appeases him. I'll play the part for now, even though I'd be a lot more concerned if they could harm him or use me against him.

I suppose they could, but they'd be signing their own death warrant. Everyone in the criminal world knows not to mess with the Hunter.

"Mom? That's the excuse you're going with?" I raise an eyebrow, squeezing his hand.

His eyes darken, making my heart beat a little faster. It's not often he gets this dark look toward me.

"Is it so wrong for me to want to keep my baby

girl safe?" he questions, taking his seat belt off and sliding across the bench seat to cup my cheek. "You, Daria, are the only thing I have ever, and will ever, care about on this earth. If something were to happen to you, I would brutally kill everyone who hurt you before burning the world to ash and taking my own life," he growls.

When I see the pure love and affection on his face, his words hit home, and my eyes begin to mist.

"I know," I whisper, leaning into his palm. "I love you too, Dad."

He sighs. "I know I can't stop you from being just like me, and I promise I will teach you everything. Just promise me you will give college your best shot and graduate. Make your mother happy that you at least have a fallback career in case you ever need it."

A fallback. He and I both know that's not even an option. I could never work a nine-to-five. I cannot stand being around mundane people on a good day, and I've come overly close to killing a few times already. Like my first boyfriend.

Though, it's not his fault, really. I knew I was gay, but Mom wasn't fully ready to accept that. I was only eight at the time, and she thought I was going through the boys have cooties stage, so she would constantly set up playdates with other kids my age.

Most of them boys. Too bad I wasn't going through a cooties phase at all.

Okay, maybe the term boyfriend is a bit too liberal, considering we were eight-years-old. He wasn't a bad person, but the second he tried to kiss me, I used the self-defence Dad had been teaching me at the cabin, hitting him in the throat with my palm.

To say I hurt him is probably an understatement. Mom was furious. Dad was proud. See? Dad and I are one and the same.

Don't worry, Mom is fully accepting of my sexual preference and orientation. She just didn't realize that an eight-year-old was fully capable of grasping and understanding who and what they were.

Now she knows. After Bethany, my only friend in high school, got pregnant at sixteen, I think she's actually glad I wasn't out hooking up with guys. But the women... there are plenty of skirts and panties in my past.

I smirk at the thought as the car pulls to a stop.

"I won't need it, Dad. Just because the world doesn't know whose daughter I am, doesn't make it any less true. I'm your kid through and through," I tell him proudly.

He chuckles gently, pulling me into a tight hug in

the back seat before whispering. "Yeah, that's what I worry about."

I scoff, pulling back to slap his chest. "You're worried about my safety."

"I am." He nods. "I was a hellion at your age. You're going to end up giving me a goddamn heart attack. I just know it," he states, rubbing at his chest and making me laugh.

"Oh, please," I say, rolling my eyes for dramatic effect. "You have a very long life ahead of you."

I make light of the conversation, but I always worry about his job. I know he's the best, but there is always an element of danger in his life. It's why Carlos drives him around in a blacked-out, bullet-proof SUV, after all.

When you're the best, there is always someone trying to knock you from that standing.

I shake off the morbid thoughts, reminding myself that he takes every precaution possible. The killer side of him doesn't even resemble who my father is to the rest of the world. To me.

The dangerous world he works in sees a man with a beard and cold brown eyes that are big enough to crush them under his palm. Even Carlos has a disguise, believe it or not.

While the world fears my father's identity as a killer, they love the man he shows in public. The clean-shaven man with soft green eyes that sparkle. The CEO of a billion-dollar tech company who donates to dozens of charities a year.

I love both sides of him because they combine to make the man that raised me, and I could never fear him.

He lives the epitome of a double life. He's safe as long as his secret is safe.

"So do you, sweetheart." He claps his large hand over my shoulder with a smirk. "And it starts by being a normal college student."

Fuck.

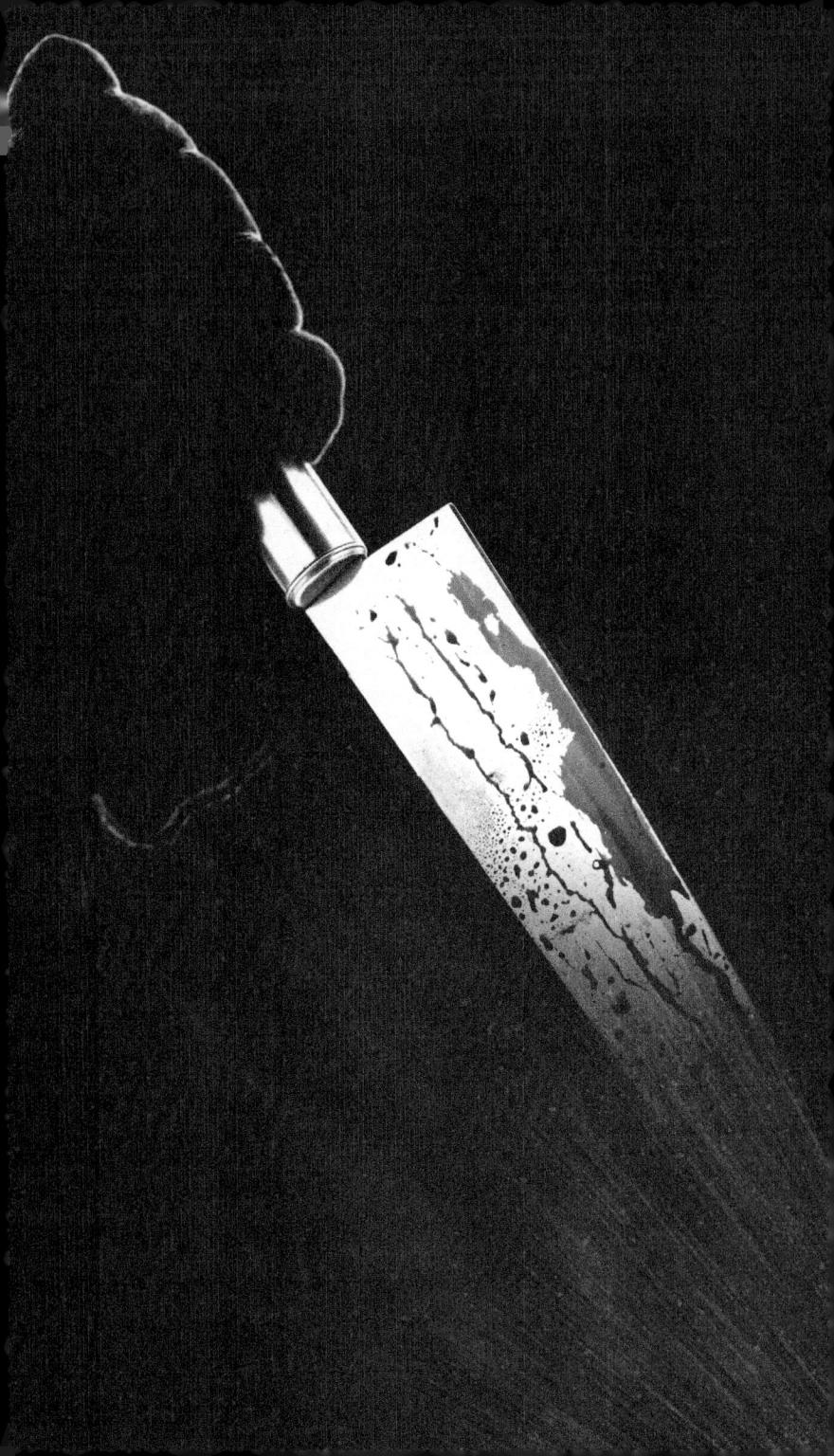

CHAPTER 2
MELANIE

C<small>RAP</small>. She still isn't here.

Maybe she got lost or switched rooms last minute? No, that can't be it otherwise housing would have notified me.

What if she doesn't like me? I've heard so many horror stories about roommates in dorms. I really don't want her to be like that. I'm already not much of a people person, so adding a horrible roommate would just make it worse.

Right, that's why you're pledging to a sorority.

Shut up, inner monologue. You're freaking annoying, and you know why I'm doing it. I'm doing it for Mom.

"But do I really want to?" I whisper into the empty room.

I got here two hours ago and quickly unpacked everything. I can't believe Dad insisted on driving us all the way here and staying in a hotel room overnight just so he could fly home tomorrow and leave the car for me.

A part of me doesn't want him to leave without me.

We both know why I chose this particular college. It's where he and Mom met and fell in love. It's where Mom found a sisterhood. One she talked about until the cancer took her from us two years ago, and one she wanted so badly for me to experience.

So, of course I came here. It was practically her dying wish for me to find that sense of family she'd had with them, and Dad agreed it would help me to have a group of women in my life.

I disagree given how antisocial I prefer to be, but still. I'm a legacy, and I can do this. It will help me feel closer to her.

"No. No, I am not going to cry," I tell myself sternly.

"I hope not. That would be one hell of a rejection to my arrival," a voice sounds from the door.

I yelp, jumping as my heart pounds. "Oh, my God! You scared me!" I squeak, turning around to look at my new roommate.

Well, I assume she's my roommate. No one else would have a key outside of the administration. Crap, I didn't even hear her come in. I need to pay more attention to my surroundings.

"Sorry," I say, shaking my head as my breath catches.

She is gorgeous. Like, drop-dead stunning. She's tall with long, dark, wavy brown hair, and she has the brightest green eyes I've ever seen.

When she smiles at me, I swear my heart stops for a fleeting moment. I've never felt an attraction to someone like this before. Sure, I've been attracted to other women, even dated a few girls in high school, but the way I felt about them is nothing compared to what I'm feeling right now.

"You're Melanie, right?" she asks.

I swallow and nod like a complete idiot, internally groaning at myself.

"Yes. Hi," I say once I've found my voice. Though, it comes out way too chipper. "You must be Daria."

"I am." She nods with a smile, still looking me over as though she's assessing me.

I don't know if I'm seeing things, but there's almost a coldness to her. No, that's not the right word. A harshness. Like she doesn't just take anything at face value. She has to study it to make sure it's up to her standards.

And that's how she's looking at me now.

"Why were you going to cry?" she asks gently, moving over to her side of the room and dropping her bag onto the floor before taking a seat on the bed.

Crap. Can't we just skip past that part?

"Uh, just thinking about things." I clear my throat, trying my best to keep the emotion out of it. The last thing I need to do is tell her about my mother. Talk about a depressing conversation starter.

She tilts her head, a worried look on her face. Oh no, did I put that there? Darn it.

"Well, we can't have you crying on your first day here," she says, standing up to fix the leather jacket she's wearing.

Her style is so different from mine. Hell, everything about her is almost the polar opposite of me. She's a couple of inches taller than me and lean. I may not be much shorter than her, but I'm a heck of a lot curvier than she is. She's smooth and curvy in all the right places, looking like she walked off the runway at some sort of edgy fashion show. Her hair is a dark brunette to my white blonde, and my eyes are blue where hers are green.

Geez. Shut up, Mel! You're being a dork.

"We can't?" I question.

Now I'm the one eyeing her suspiciously. She has this sparkle in her eye that promises mischief.

"Nope, we can't," she says cheerfully, taking me off guard as she moves to stand before me. "And I have just the thing to cheer you up."

I blink. Uh-oh. "You do, huh?" I go with being a little flirty instead of outright asking her what exactly she has planned.

"Dinner. We definitely need to go out for dinner."

Oh. Well, I'm sure Dad would be fine with her joining us, and he might feel better seeing her. He is so worried I would end up having a rude roommate, and Daria doesn't seem rude at all. Calculated and untrusting, maybe, but definitely not rude.

"I actually have plans to meet up with my dad for dinner. Would you like to come?" I ask, feeling a little awkward.

"I don't want to intrude," she says quickly, but I chuckle and shake my head.

"Not at all! He's flying home tomorrow, but he wanted to meet you and make sure you weren't a serial killer or something." I giggle at the joke, and she laughs awkwardly.

"No way. That would be scary, right?" She laughs it off, and I snort.

"Pretty sure the college does extensive background checks to avoid that, but you know dads."

Something I can't decipher flashes in her eyes before she smiles.

"Tell me about it. My father is wickedly paranoid about my safety," she tells me, and I breathe a sigh of relief. For a moment, I was worried I had put my foot in my mouth.

"Are you from D.C.?" I ask her, fighting the urge to reach out and touch her. I don't understand why I'm so attracted to her.

Okay, I do. She's freaking gorgeous, but touching her would definitely put me on the creeper scale when we've just met.

"My mom lives not too far from here actually," she says, her expression guarded.

"I'm sorry. It's none of my business and I'm being no—"

"No! No, it's just… there's something about you that has me wanting to spill all of my secrets," she whispers, looking completely confused.

"Oh," I whisper back, feeling myself blush.

"Damn, that's cute," she comments, and I blush harder. "I'm not really used to telling people about my life. I'm more of a lone wolf type," she explains.

I don't know why I'm a little disappointed. I

mean, technically, I'm not one to have a lot of friends either. People give me anxiety.

My phone rings before I can respond, and I know it's my dad. "That would be Dad. He's probably hungry." I laugh, grabbing the phone off my nightstand. "Hey, Dad."

"Hi, darling. Have you met your roomie yet?" he asks, trying to sound cool, and it makes me smile.

My eyes move to Daria. "Yeah, she's pretty cool. Would you be alright with me bringing her along?" I ask him, already knowing his answer.

I quickly put him on speaker so she can hear it from him. I don't want her to think she's intruding.

"Of course! Bring her along, my treat!" he says, sounding thrilled, and she relaxes.

"Okay, great! We'll meet you there in half an hour, Dad. Love you," I tell him.

"Love you too, darling. See you soon and drive safe. None of that crazy driving you like to partake in, alright? I'd rather not have a heart attack while I'm this young," he says before hanging up the phone.

Daria breaks into laughter, shaking her head. When she sees me watching her, she laughs even harder, reaching out to grab my arm to steady herself.

"Sorry. Sorry, it's just… my old man dropped me

off and accused me of the same thing," she explains, and I can't help but laugh with her.

"They're so overprotective," I giggle, enjoying the feel of her hand on my arm. It's comforting for reasons I don't understand.

Maybe Mom was right. Maybe I do need to let more people get close to me.

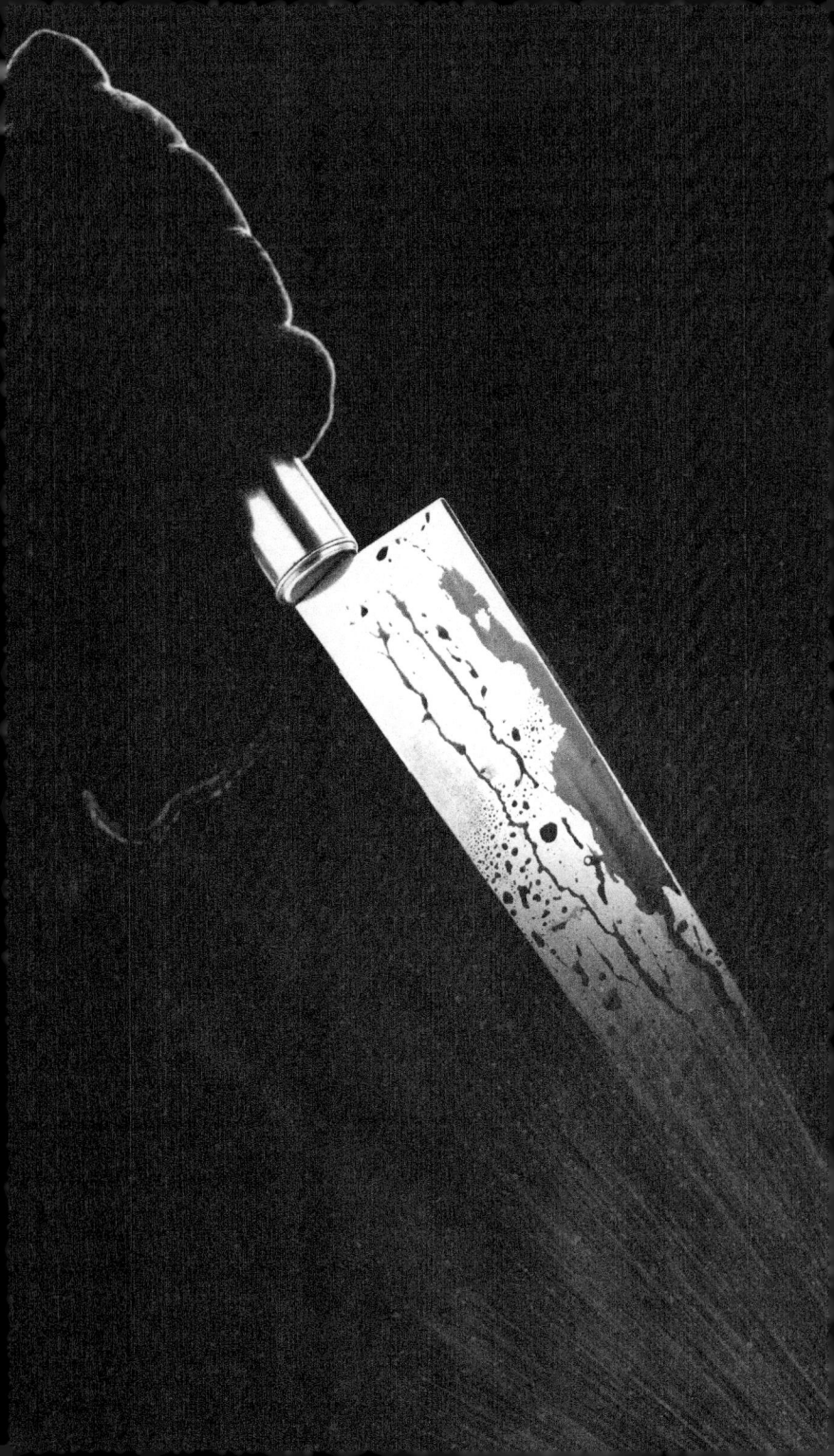

CHAPTER 3
DARIA

This may just be the most awkward thing I've done in a while.

Why I agreed to go to dinner with Melanie and her father is escaping me, but I just couldn't bring myself to tell her no. There's something about her that just seems so pure and untouched by the darkness in life.

She hasn't lived in the world I intend to thrive in, where violence and death are second nature. She's like a breath of fresh air in a way.

"Daria, what does your father do for a living?" Mr. Mahone asks me after we've finished eating.

I smile. "He works with a bunch of tech stuff," I tell him, used to the half lie sliding from my lips.

Even as the CEO billionaire, no one knows he has

a daughter. Dad has taken every single precaution to keep me safe in case his identity was ever found out.

"Oh, that sounds interesting," Melanie says, and I soften toward her excitement. Just a little.

"I guess." I shrug, pretending like I'm not overly interested in anything Dad does, even though I absorb it all from killing to computers and everything in between.

Mr. Mahone chuckles, and I excuse myself to the bathroom, shooting a text off to Dad on his secure phone.

> ME:
> I'm almost done with dinner. My new roommate is… sweet. She even made a joke about her dad worrying I was a serial killer :)

> DAD:
> Well, that's an interesting opener. Do you like her? I can still get you that apartment if you'd prefer.

I smile down at my phone. Even when he's halfway around the country on a job, he's still thinking of me.

> ME:
> You just left this afternoon. Don't worry about me. I'm fine. ;)

DAD:

You know how to reach me if you need me. Gotta go. Love you, sweetheart.

ME:

Love you, Dad. Be safe.

DAD:

Always, kid.

I snort, shoving the phone back into my pocket as I head back to their table, stopping when Melanie sounds frustrated.

"Of course, I like her, Dad."

"I think she has eyes for you, too, darling."

That has my eyes widening. I wouldn't say I have eyes for her, not really. As beautiful as she is, she's too sweet to get mixed up with someone like me.

"Daddy, I know you met Mom and fell in love while you were here, but this isn't some sort of magical place. I just met her, and she's my roommate." She sighs heavily. "And we can't forget that we don't even know if she likes girls. It's complicated."

She sounds a little sad, and I find myself not liking that much. I also love women, but that's a complete other conversation between her and me for a later time.

I feel a bit awkward standing here when I know I shouldn't be eavesdropping, but I'd rather wait out this tension than come back right in the middle of it.

"I know, but don't close your heart and mind off to the possibilities. Your mother wanted you to come here to experience life. You've got to go out there and try. She'd want you to," he tells her, and I feel bad.

It's clear her mom is no longer alive. I can't even imagine the pain of losing a parent.

"I know, Dad. I promise you, I'll open up. I'm pledging next week," she says in a cheery voice, but when I walk around the corner, it's easy to tell the smile doesn't reach her eyes.

"Did I just hear you say you're pledging?" I ask, feeling a little nauseated. Sorority girls aren't known for being the nicest. Unless you're like them, and I can already tell she isn't.

She blushes again, and fuck, it really is cute how easily she gets flustered.

"Uh, yeah. I'm a legacy, and I promised my mom I would give it a go. She says it was the best years of her life." The pain in her voice is heartbreaking. I wish I could comfort her, but that's really not my area of expertise.

Pain and agony? Totally. Insane sexual pleasure? I'm your girl. But being caring toward someone that isn't my parents is something I'm not used to, but I think I'd like to try… for her.

"You'll do great, Mel," her dad says gently.

Melanie nods as she blinks a few times to stop her tears from falling, but I see them.

"Hey, he's right," I say, reaching my hand over to tap hers. It's a gesture Mom uses on me when I'm upset about something. I find it comforting in those times, so maybe she will too. "If it's something you want, I bet you'll really enjoy it."

"Any chance you'd want to join me?" she asks, and I choke.

"Yeah, that's going to be a pass for me." I wave my hand down my body, pointing out the leather jacket, ripped jeans, and biker boots. "Not exactly the sorority type."

I'm sure there's a sorority for everyone. I'm not saying they stick to the conventional stereotypes depicted in movies and shit, but still. Unless they have a sorority where they teach you how to harness and hone your skills in order to become a lethal killer, I'm really not their type.

"Oh, good point." She nods, and I can't help but laugh.

Playing hurt, I grip my chest. "Ouch, that really hurt," I tell her, but the second her lips twitch we all burst into laughter.

Maybe coming out to dinner tonight wasn't so bad after all.

———

"Thanks for coming out with us," Melanie says once we're settled back in our dorm.

It didn't take me long to unpack everything. Considering I have daily access to Dad's penthouse and Mom's place, there wasn't much I had to bring. I will slowly move things over as I need them. It's just easier that way.

"Thank you for inviting me." I smile over at her. "It was a lot of fun, and we got to put your dad's mind at ease."

She sighs happily. "Yeah, I'm glad. He worries too much now that Mom is gone." Her voice fades away at the end when she realizes she let that slip.

"Well, any time he needs a reminder that you're in good hands, send him my way." I wink, trying to lighten the mood a little before going in with the rest. "I'm sorry you lost your mom. I know it's probably not something you want to talk about, but if you ever do, I've been told I'm a good listener."

"Thanks. Maybe someday I will take you up on that."

"Okay." I smile, flopping down on my bed. "So,

want to watch a movie?"

"Depends. What exactly are you in the mood for?" she questions me, completely serious.

"I don't know. What do you want to watch?" I ask her. I don't really care what we watch, I just need something to zone out on before I go to sleep. Going down a TikTok rabbit-hole while being antisocial seems a little rude when we've just met.

"What's your favourite movie?" she asks instead, and I have to think about it.

"I don't have one." I shrug. "I'm very much a mood watcher. Some days it's movies like Die Hard, and some days it's movies like Something Borrowed."

"Okay, you pass the test," she says in all seriousness.

"There's a test?" I raise an eyebrow in question.

"Of course, there's a test. I take movies very seriously. If you can't be open to different types, we can't be friends." She nods like she's some snooty princess, and I fall over laughing.

"I—oh my, God." I laugh harder, clutching my stomach as she smiles at me. "You're a movie snob!" I point out, and she shrugs.

"We all have our burdens. This is mine," she says with a serious face before laughing along with me.

I think I may have just made a lifelong friend.

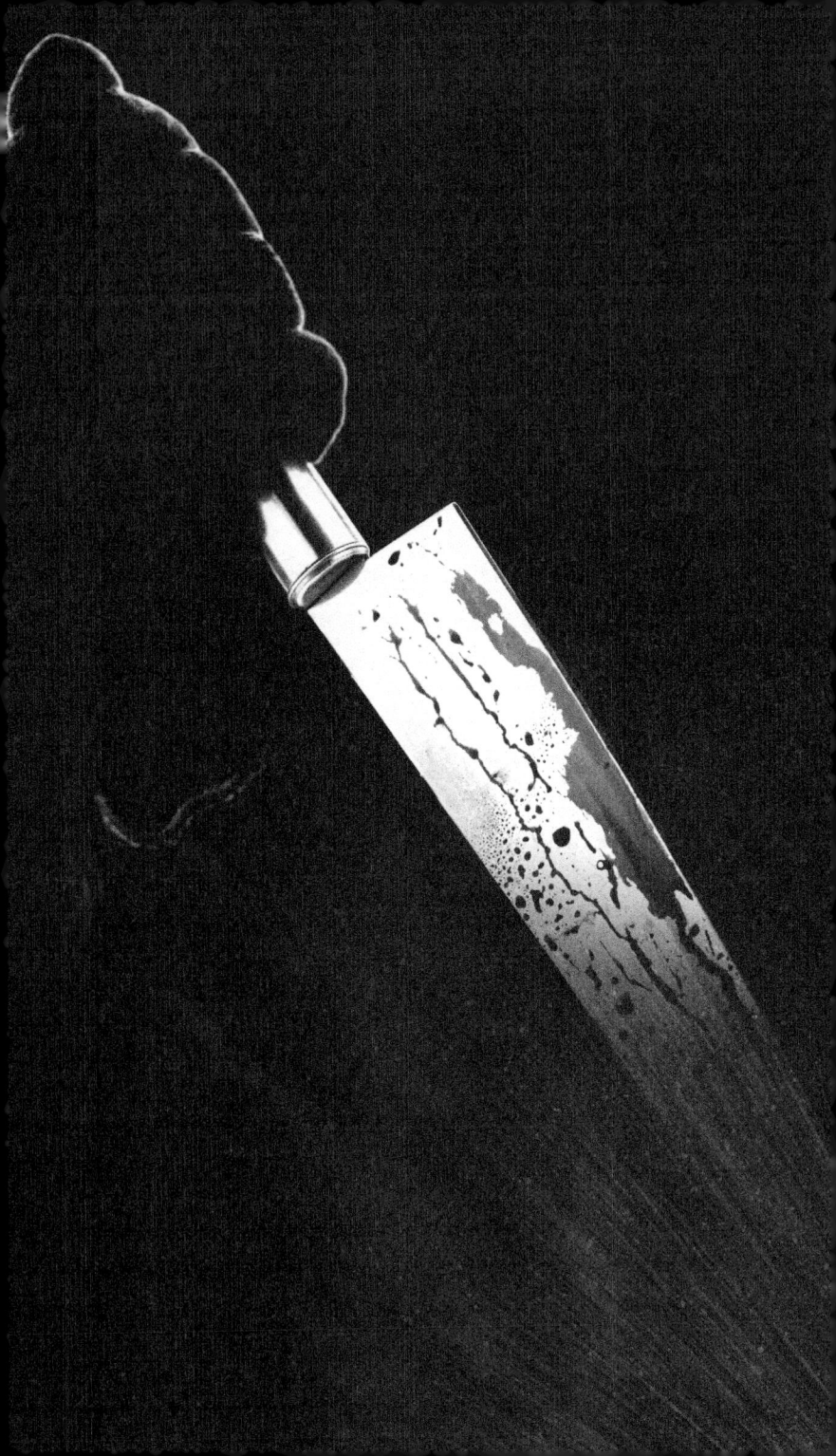

CHAPTER 4
DARIA

APPARENTLY, when my new roommate doesn't get enough sleep, she's cranky, and it's fucking adorable. She's like an angry kitten with a scowl on her face, trying to get ready for the first class of the day.

Me? I'm used to it. I've always been a night owl, and I don't see that changing anytime soon.

"How can you just be so chipper?" she grumbles at me, making me laugh.

No one has ever accused me of being chipper before. "I'm not chipper. I just don't require as much sleep as most. Why didn't you tell me you didn't handle staying up late very well? We could have stopped after one movie," I tell her.

She groans, looking a little embarrassed. "Because I didn't want to seem like a child. I'm sad Dad left this morning, and I was having a good time watching movies to take my mind off of it."

As her words sink in, I feel like a jackass for not thinking about the possibility of her being upset. I guess I take it for granted that I still have both of my parents and that they live close to me. I can't even imagine how she's feeling.

Swallowing down the thickness at even the idea of not having my parents around, I nod. "Sorry. I guess I didn't really think before speaking."

She smiles, but it doesn't reach her eyes as she throws her bag over her shoulder. "It's okay. I'm not the only student here that moved away from their parents," she says, and I nod.

I don't point out the truth in that statement or that she could very well be the only one who lost one parent in the past few years who just moved away from the other. Instead, I do the only thing that comes to mind.

Walking over to her, I pull her into a hug. For a split second, I think I made a huge mistake by not asking her for permission first, but that thought disappears when she melts into me. Her arms wrap around my waist as she takes a deep, calming breath.

"I can't imagine the position you're in, but I could see the sadness in your eyes when your dad dropped us off last night," I tell her, giving her one more squeeze before easing back and resting my hands on her shoulders. "All I can tell you is the distance does get easier."

She sniffles, nodding as her eyes catch mine. "You have experience in that arena?" she asks quietly, and I inwardly wince. There's a fine line between what I can and cannot tell her where Dad is concerned, but I decide on the bare minimum truth. Even then, it's more than I've ever told anyone else.

"My Dad travels a lot for his job, and my parents were never together." I shrug. "I only get to see him occasionally," I tell her.

It's a white lie. While he may travel a lot, I also see him often. I don't think we've ever gone more than a week without seeing each other face-to-face. He's always been very hands on in raising me. Another thing I take for granted.

Fuck. I'm not really enjoying being so aware of my own emotions. It's weird for me to feel shit.

"Oh," she says in shock, her eyes widening before she frowns. Pity. That's the look I see on her face, and I wish I hadn't said anything. "I'm sorry. I can't imagine what that's like. Dad was always there for me."

Mine is too, but I can't exactly backtrack now. "It's really okay. I'm lucky Mom even tracked him down when she didn't have to." I shrug again, grabbing my own bag for class. "And he loves me. That's more than a lot of people can say, right?"

"Yeah, that's true, I guess," she says. "Alright, let's get this day started. What is your first class?" she asks me, moving to open the door and changing the subject.

Thank fuck.

"Intro to Coding," I tell her, and she scrunches her nose.

"That sounds... never mind. I'll stick to my Intro to Philosophy class," she says, making me laugh.

"I like numbers." I smile widely as I close and lock the door. "Besides, learning code is something that can always be useful."

"Glad to know who the brainiac is in this friendship," she teases, and I snort.

"Philosophy isn't exactly for schmucks either, miss smartie pants," I tease back, making her giggle.

I can honestly say I've never met someone that giggled where it wasn't a show or ploy to garner someone's attention. When Melanie does it naturally, it doesn't grate on my nerves, and I find it's adorable on her.

"Fine, we're both smart." She smiles, and I nod, bumping my shoulder into hers.

She's shorter than me by a couple of inches, so it's

more like the top of my arm to her shoulder, but close enough.

I actually enjoy that she isn't that much shorter than me. I also love the fact that she's soft and curvaceous everywhere, but that line of thought will only turn me on, and I won't be able to focus in class if I'm thinking about her.

"Yes, we are." I agree with her, pausing when I have to part from her. "See you tonight?"

"Yeah. I'll be late. I have to go over to sorority row for this mixer they're throwing. It's for anyone interested in pledging," she tells me shyly.

Okay, that's good. It will give me time to hit the shooting range after classes let out.

"That sounds fun…" I say, smiling when she laughs.

"I'm sure it will be." She loses the smile on her face. "Mom loved being a part of a sisterhood, and she wanted me to experience that. It's the least I can do for her," she says quietly.

Another piece of the puzzle that is Melanie forms in my mind as we part and head to our classes.

Now I know why I didn't peg her for much of a sorority girl. She isn't doing it as something she necessarily wants, but as a way to feel closer to her mom. I really hope she finds that peace and sense of belonging.

And while she's off doing whatever happens at those things, I will be shooting targets, working on perfecting my already impressive aim. The more accurate the shot, the more deadly I will be.

Bring on the fun.

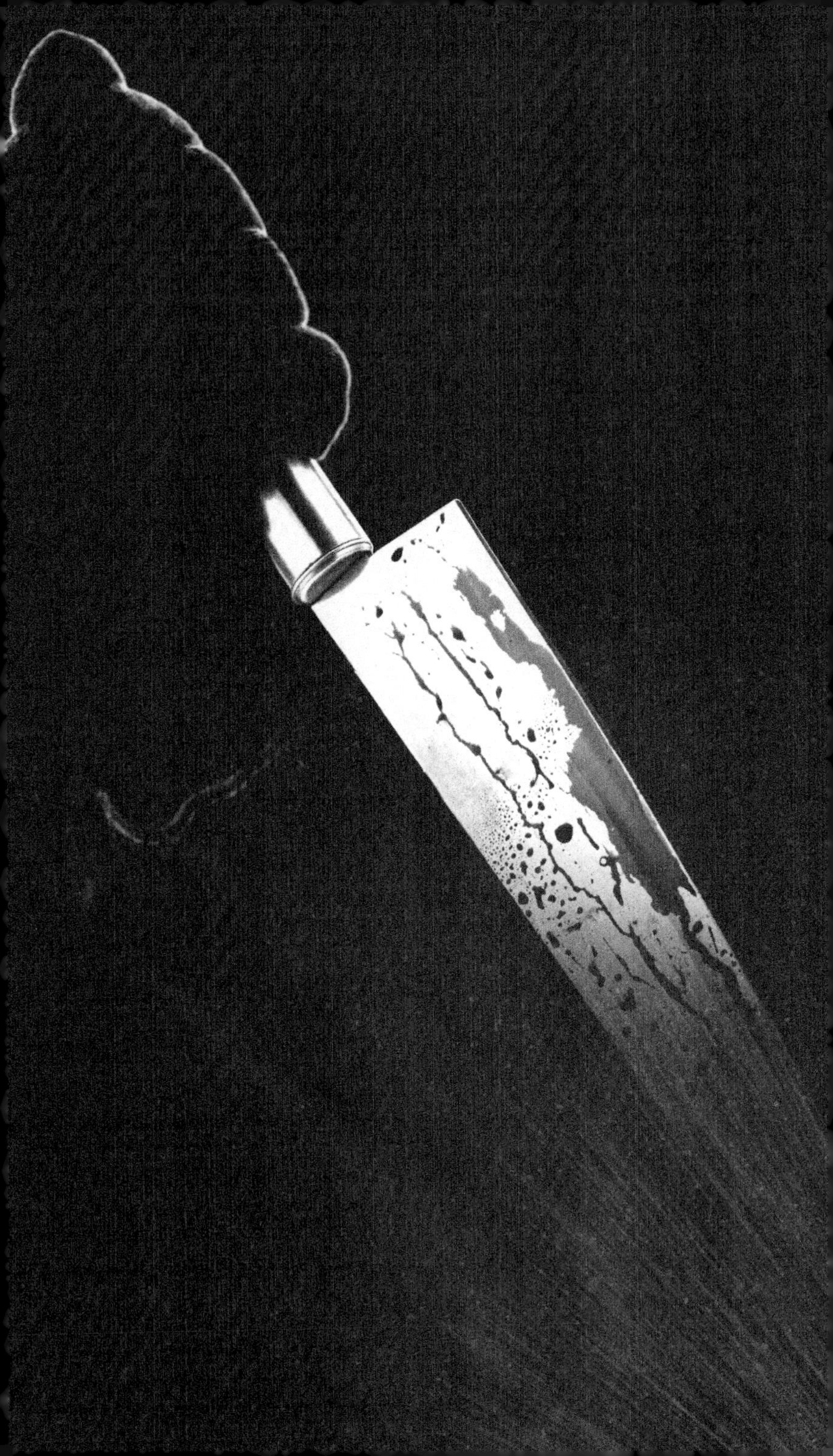

CHAPTER 5
MELANIE

When Mom said this was the best time of her life, I wasn't really expecting… well, this.

Some of the sororities and frats seem so welcoming and inclusive, but not this one. *Beta Delta Phi* feels more like a social experiment gone wrong, and not the loving sisterhood Mom spoke of.

I guess it's probably changed a lot since she was here. In reality, it probably changes often as new girls come in and others graduate. That's just the natural way of things, but this wasn't what I had in mind.

I was already skeptical of joining because I'm not really a socially outgoing person. Not that it's a requirement, but it would probably help. Now, seeing how the sorority my mom loved is very clique centred, I'm really beginning to regret my choice to come here.

You owe it to your mom, Mel. You can do this. Besides, you're judging them before you've even given them a chance. That makes you no better than them if they turn out to be who you think they are.

I sigh, hating this inner conflict I'm having. Of course, I want to make my mother happy, and this was always so important to her. I know my feelings would mean just as much to her, but if she were still here, I know she would tell me to give it an honest chance first.

"Excuse me," a girl with bright red hair—that's clearly fake—stops in front of me.

"Yes?" I ask, instantly recognizing the symbol on her shirt. I let out a nervous breath and put a smile on my face. "Hi, I'm Melanie." I put my hand out to shake hers, but all she does is look down at it with disdain.

"Right," she says, still staring at my hand like it has somehow offended her. "I think you're in the wrong place," she tells me, moving her cold eyes back to mine.

I suck in a sharp breath, momentarily scared of her, before shaking myself out of it. I've dealt with more than one mean girl in my life. Surely, I can handle this one too.

"Actually, I'm right where I'm supposed to be. My mother was a member a long time ago," I say sweetly, refusing to let the pain of losing her show and offer up a vulnerability to this girl.

"You're a legacy?" she gasps, and I smile.

"I am. I was just coming to check everything out," I tell her, looking around at the others gathered around.

A group of guys from *Alpha Kappa Phi*—the frat connected to *Beta Delta Phi*—are watching us as they stand with a few of the other girls I saw earlier with the redhead now in front of me. There's something about the way they're looking at us that makes me uneasy, but I can't place it.

"Excuse me for saying this," she hedges, "but you don't exactly look the sorority type."

I almost snort at just how right she is, but I don't.

"Thank you for your concern," I say sarcastically, unable to help myself.

She narrows her eyes at me. "You don't need to be rude."

"Neither do you. I haven't done anything to you, and you're already trying to warn me against pledging. Why?" I question, already anticipating her answer.

"Look, it's nothing personal, but we have an image to uphold. You don't fit that bill." The level of righteous attitude coming from her grates on my nerves.

"Are you a legacy—" I ask her, waving my hand and making it known I trailed off because I don't know her name.

"Deedra, and no." She sticks her nose in the air.

"Well, I am, and I would like to pledge," I tell her, making up my mind. I'm not going to let some mean girl get in the way of feeling closer to my mom.

She looks at me with a hatred in her eyes that makes me lose the small amount of confidence I had. Just because I'm a legacy doesn't mean I truly belong here. And if they don't want me to join them, they'll find a way to make my life a living hell until I give up.

"Sign-up table is over there." She points at the table I've already been to.

"Thank you." I take a deep, calming breath. "Look, I think we got off on the wrong foot. I tend to get grouchy when I haven't slept well," I explain to her. "My mother died a couple of years ago, and it was her dying wish that I join. I need to at least give it a shot for her."

She assesses me for a moment before nodding. "I get that, but you really don't seem like you want to be here," she says.

"I'm nervous. You're also not helping me feel at ease by insinuating that I don't belong," I say quietly, wishing I hadn't come at all.

She doesn't say anything else, just leaves me alone and returns to the group of people that were watching our entire interaction.

Feeling drained, I decide to call it a day and head back to the dorm. At least I have a friendly face waiting for me there.

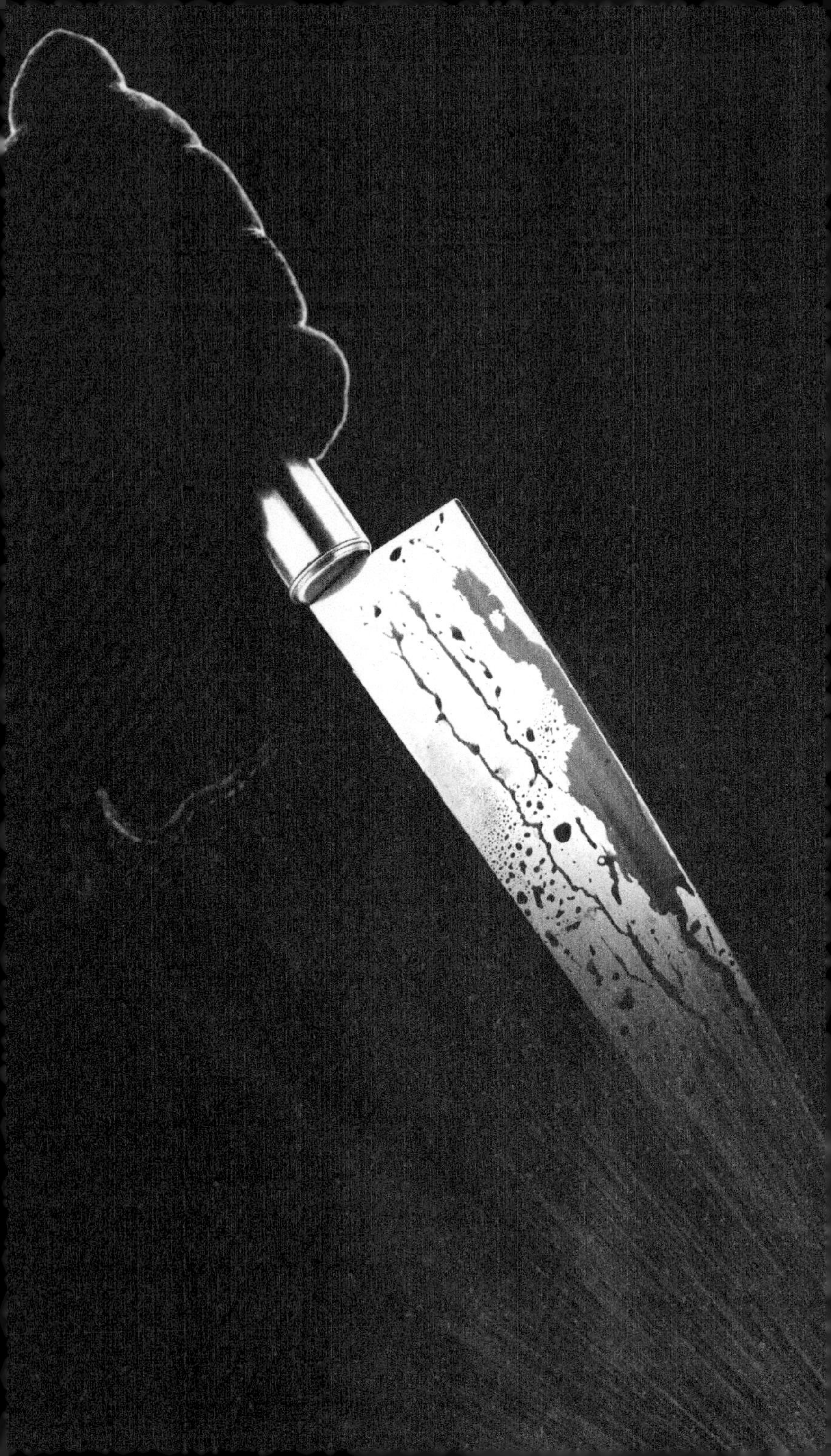

CHAPTER 6
DARIA

By the time I leave the shooting range, I'm starving. I know the dorm doesn't have any food, so I head to Dad's penthouse, calling him on the way.

"Daria, everything okay, sweetheart?" he asks through the speakers of the car.

"Yeah, just letting you know I'm going to the apartment for something to eat. Didn't want you to worry when your phone notified you," I tell him, navigating the streets downtown.

"Why aren't you at school?" he questions me, and I roll my eyes.

"I went to the range after class."

His sigh is long and drawn out. "You know I have a range in the basement of the building. Why do you insist on using the public one, possibly putting yourself in danger?" he barks down the line.

"We've been over this, Dad. I prefer the public one. That way, no one questions who I am or how I learned to shoot so well." I've been adamant about it since he taught me how to shoot at the cabin when I was seven.

If I only used his private ranges, it would raise a lot of suspicion if the wrong person caught wind of my talents. This way, I have a public record of my growing skill, and it won't raise suspicion with anyone in the criminal underworld if they happened to catch wind of it.

To anyone around me, I'm just another scared little girl wanting to protect herself from the big bad men of the world. Shooting also relaxes me. I know it's weird, but knowing I have deadly accuracy with any gun helps me feel safe. Or safer, I guess.

"And I have told you they scout those places looking for unclaimed talent. It's a risk for you to go there and shoot the way you do," he says into the phone, no anger in his voice. Just concern for my safety.

"Don't worry, Dad. I watch just how accurate I am when I'm there. I don't work hard to be the dead-on shooter we both know I am. I take precautions. I just wanted to practice and take the edge off." I wince as soon as the words are out of my mouth.

"Edge off of what, Daria?" he questions, his voice

deadly calm as I pull into the underground parking garage of his building.

"Nothing important," I groan, trying not to get into this conversation with him. He will tell me the same thing he always does when it comes to letting people close. Innocents don't belong in our world. We must distance ourselves from them. It's the best way to keep them safe and unaware.

"Everything to do with you is important, sweetheart," he grumbles. I can hear him moving some papers around wherever he is. "It can't be school already."

I laugh, parking the car I borrowed earlier to get to the range. "No, it's not school. Not really, anyhow."

There's a silence over the line as he thinks over my words before he speaks again.

"Is this a sex thing?" he asks gently, and I groan.

"No. No, Dad, we are not going there," I remind him. "I already had to talk to Mom a million times about this shit. I'm not doing it with you, too." I smirk, knowing he's annoyed that I refuse to talk to him openly about this one area of my life.

We talk about everything together, but I draw the line when it comes to my sex life. And his if you want to get technical. He can see me as his sweet little girl that never has sex, and I can think of him as a monk. It's a win-win.

"Fine, fine." He gives in easily, and I breathe out a sigh of relief. Thank fuck for that. "Are you spending the night at the apartment?" he questions instead.

A part of me wants to because my bed here is literally heaven, but I know I can't really get used to being at college if I'm not doing the entire college experience. I also never swapped numbers with Melanie, and I told her I would be back tonight.

"No. I just need to eat something and then I'm taking the bus back."

He growls. "I do not like you taking public transit. It isn't safe."

"It's perfectly safe," I growl back.

"Do you know how many people I have killed in public, Daria?" he asks me, reminding me just how deadly he is.

"I try not to think about it. Kind of ruins the whole experience I like to call life," I snark back. I'm aware of the surrounding dangers, but I also refuse to let him wrap me in bubble wrap.

"You could get mugged."

"I wish them luck. I can disarm a man your size in two seconds flat," I remind him.

"Raped," he counters.

"I have my knives. I would castrate the bastard before he had a chance."

He sighs, annoyed by my persistence. "I am more than aware of your ability to keep yourself safe."

"Then why are you worrying so much? Normal people can die just by stepping outside of their houses," I remind him gently.

"You are not normal, Daria. You're my world. Remember what I said in the car yesterday. If something were to happen to you, I would burn the entire world down until there was nothing left."

I smile into the darkness of the car, even though he can't see me. "I know, Daddy. But I promise you, I'm safe."

"I want you to take the blue Honda in the garage," he says, tapping away on his computer. "I already set it up for you to have campus parking, but you were too stubborn to take me up on the offer before."

I groan, hating how overprotective he is. Does he not realize how rare it is for first year college students to have their own vehicles? I'm trying to keep a low profile here.

"Dad," I start, but he doesn't let me finish.

"No, Daria. I would prefer you have a vehicle at your disposal in case of emergencies."

I frown at that. "Emergencies?" I question. Not

once in my life have I ever heard Dad use that term before. He always says emergencies are for life and death matters only, so now I'm worried.

"Well, that's what we're going to tell your mother it's for. But I'd like you to be able to go wherever you need to, maybe even start helping me on a few jobs in the city," he says, and my heart skips a beat.

"You want to start training me? I thought you said that I had to graduate first." I can hear the excitement in my own voice, and Dad chuckles.

"Daria, sweetheart, I have technically been training you your entire life. But no. I am not getting you to help me with contracts, but I might want to test your sleuthing skills. Killing is only a small part of this job."

Hell, even that has me excited. I thought he was going to keep me from doing anything until after I graduated. He wants me to spy on some marks before he makes his move? I'm there.

"Okay," I say, trying to sound calm. By the way he laughs, I know I failed miserably, but I can't even be mad about it.

"Deal?" he asks, making sure I'm paying attention.

"My agreement to take the blue Honda in exchange for you pulling me in to help you with certain assignments, as boring as you believe them to be? Yeah, you've got a deal."

"Good. Let me know when you get back to the dorms tonight. Love you, kid," he says into the phone. I can tell by the tone of his voice that he's smiling.

He's probably gloating over the fact that he won this round since I'm taking the car back to school. I should be pissed that he was able to manipulate me so easily, but I can't find it in me to care.

"Love you too, Dad."

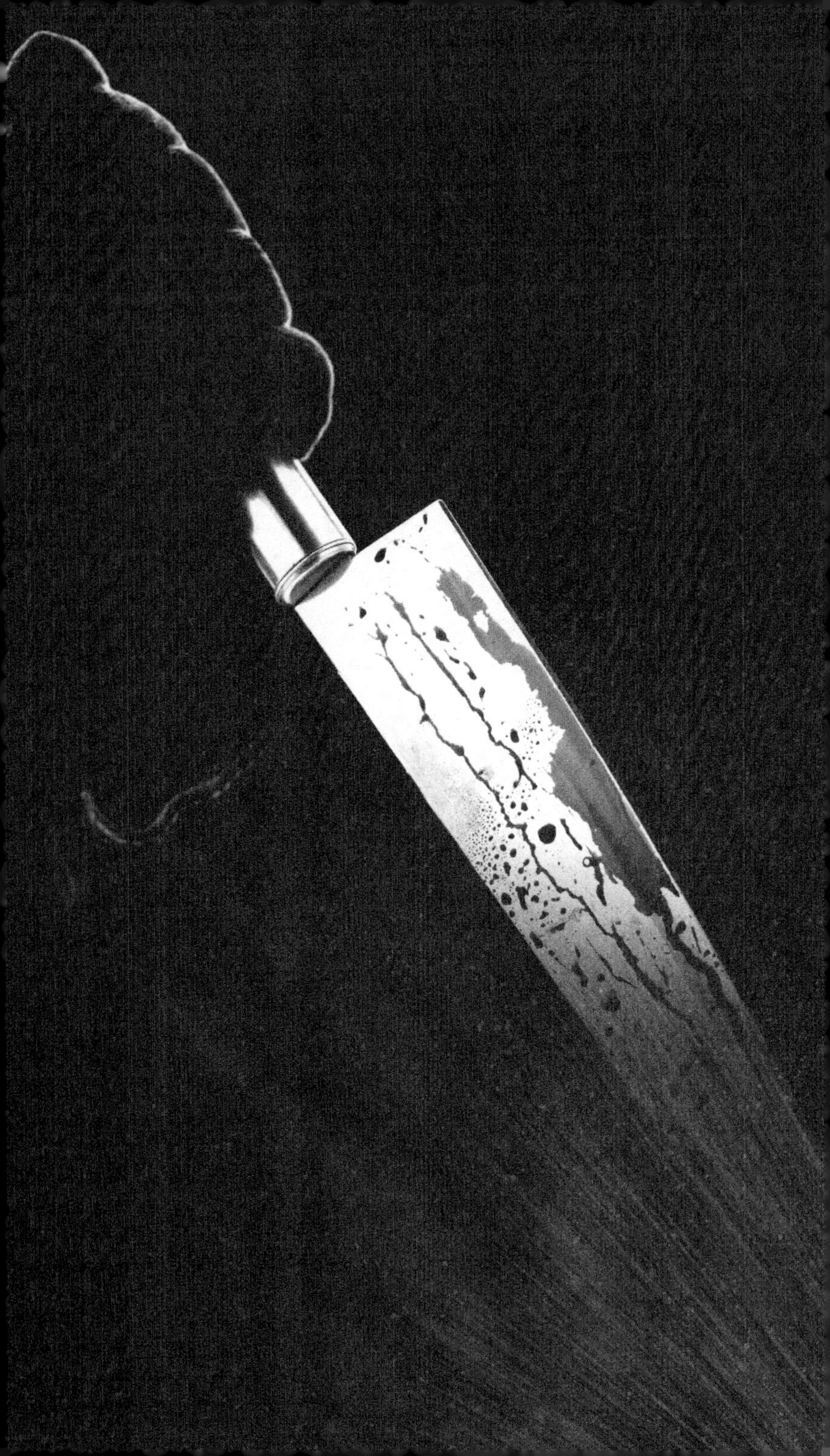

CHAPTER 7
MELANIE

"Dammit," I curse under my breath when I stub my toe on something. I'm too distracted with how hot Daria looks when she walks out of the bathroom in booty shorts and a tank top.

"You okay?" Daria asks, coming to my side like I'd hurt my head rather than my freaking ego.

"Haven't really learned how to walk yet," I tell her, laughing it off the best I can.

I've been in a mood since I left that mixer, and the longer I think about it, the more angry and annoyed I get. When I got back to the room, I was actually glad Daria hadn't returned yet. It gave me a bit of time to decompress.

She chuckles softly, bending down to get a closer look at my toe. It's throbbing like a mofo, but I refuse to let on how much of a wimp I am, especially when I can feel her breath against my collarbone.

Please don't let her notice my nipples. Please don't let her notice my nipples.

"It will probably bruise a bit, but it doesn't look like you broke anything," she says, moving her head back up.

I stop breathing when her nose touches mine by accident, and she freezes.

"You, ah, know a lot about breaks?" I ask, my voice clearly breathy as I watch her lick her lips.

"Enough. Wasn't exactly the safest child growing up." Her eyes move to my lips and time seems to stand still. For a split second, I think she's going to kiss me. I hope she kisses me, but she doesn't. Instead, she pulls away, and a wave of disappointment washes over me.

Clearing my throat, I nod. "I was definitely a safe child. Didn't stop me from getting hurt, though, since I'm clumsy as all hell," I tell her, moving onto the bed and pulling the covers over my body.

She stares at me for what feels like a lifetime before looking away. Something crosses her face, but I barely know her so I can't pinpoint what it was. Disappointment? Disgust? Confusion? It could be any of them.

"You sound like my mom," she says with a laugh

as she shuts the room light off and moves into her own bed.

Our lamps are still emitting a soft glow around the room, and she turns around so she's facing me.

"Your mom is clumsy?" I ask, turning to lie on my side and face her as well. I'm not ready to say goodnight yet. She's helping me forget about everything that happened earlier.

"Dad liked to joke when I was a kid. Said he was thankful I didn't inherit her clumsiness, or he would have had to wrap me in bubble wrap," she tells me with a smile.

My heart pangs a little at the picture she's painting with her words, but I have to remind myself that her upbringing wasn't the same as mine. While she loves both parents, they were never a solid family unit like mine was growing up. Dad and I are still solid, and I wouldn't give that up for anything.

"Sounds like you lucked out then," I tell her with a smile that she easily returns.

"Definitely. I don't think I would have enjoyed life nearly as much if everything I loved to do ended up hurting me."

That has me wondering exactly what it is she likes to do to enjoy life. Not that it's any of my business.

"I will settle for leaving the dark and crazy stuff

to you, then." I laugh, and she gets a very serious expression on her face.

"Don't do anything dangerous, Mel," she tells me sternly, and my heart rate picks up.

"I wouldn't. It's not really my thing. I didn't get this cushy ass by being a daredevil. I prefer to stay inside where I'm comfy and safe," I breathe out, trying to make a joke to lighten the mood. The protective vibes she's giving off are making it hard to breathe.

"While I'm glad you don't do anything to put yourself in harm's way," she says, pushing herself up onto her elbow so she can get a better view of me. "I really don't like you talking down about yourself either." Holy fuck.

"Uh," I whisper, unable to find words right now.

"You're gorgeous, Mel. You have to know that." Her eyes darken, and she licks her lips again.

Holy shit. Is she checking me out?

"I—thank you," I say, feeling myself blush. I may not fully believe her words, but she makes me want to. I don't feel like there's some hidden message behind them like there are with so many others.

"You could be so beautiful if you just lost a bit of weight."

"You're so pretty, but don't you think you should take care of yourself?"

"Oh, honey, men would find you so attractive if you just lost some of that softness."

Yet, hearing and seeing Daria tell me she thinks I'm gorgeous? It feels genuine, with no 'buts' hanging in the air.

"You're welcome. And just so you're aware, I don't talk out of my ass either. I'm blunt to a fucking fault with absolutely no filter. I will always be straight with you," she says, closing her eyes. "If I can't be for any reason, I'll tell you I can't talk about it. I don't make it a habit of lying to my friends. Not that I really have any."

I try to keep the shock off my face.

"You don't have friends?" I ask, trying not to pry in case it's a sore subject.

"Not really. I have some people I could loosely call acquaintances, but no one I'd even miss if I were to up and move. I don't usually get attached to people," she says quietly, reaching over to shut her lamp off and burrow under the blankets.

I follow suit, getting comfortable as I ruminate on her words before speaking.

"Can I ask why?" I whisper, too curious for my own good.

"I just don't really like people. I tolerate them on a good day, but for the most part, I prefer to be by myself." A heavy silence hangs in the air before she sighs. "We should think about exchanging numbers," she says, completely changing the subject.

The change of pace shocks me back into reality, and I nod even though she can't see me in the dark room. "Yeah, that's probably a smart idea."

It is. It's something we should have done this morning in case either of us happened to forget our key to the room, or really anything. Not having a way to contact your roommate isn't overly smart.

"Goodnight, Mel," she tells me.

"Night, Daria."

After a while, I think she's fallen asleep because the room is quiet, when I hear her whisper. "I think you're going to be my first real friend, and that scares me."

The raw panic I hear in her voice confuses me. Why would being my friend be so scary to her?

"Don't be scared. It's going to be great." I add some pep to my voice, hoping to ease her worry.

"Yeah, it will, Mel. Night."

I say goodnight back. As I start to drift off to sleep, I have to wonder. Why did that sound more like a warning than a compliment?

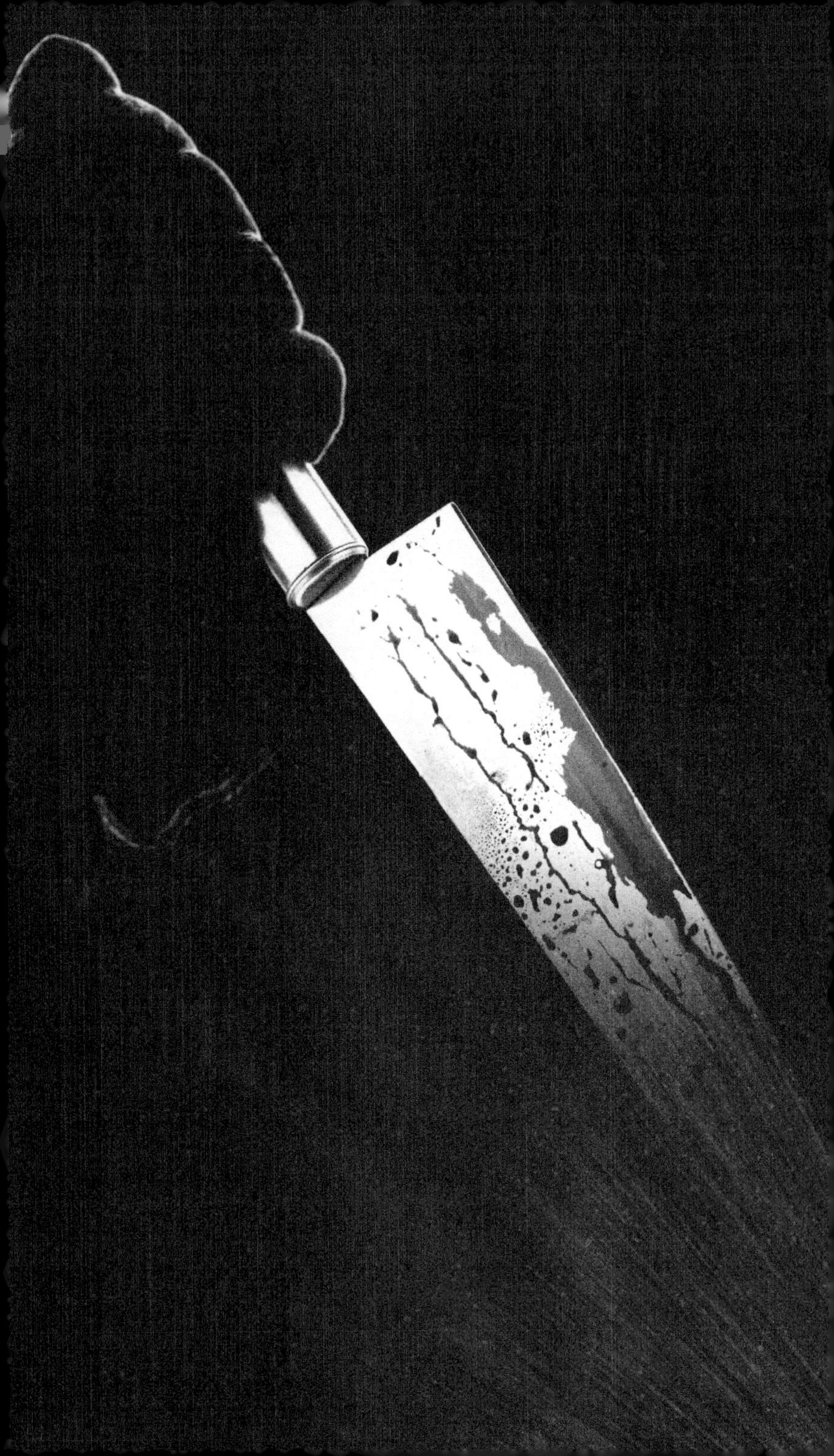

CHAPTER 8
DARIA

Mel hasn't been a little off all day, and I have the sneaking suspicion it has something to do with that mixer she attended yesterday. Not only was she down on herself, but she sort of swore.

Now, I'm fully aware that I barely know her, but saying dammit when she stubbed her toe last night was the closest thing to a curse word I've heard come out of her mouth since we met.

"What are the leading signs of a psychopath?" the professor asks the class, and everyone puts their hand up, but I don't bother.

"They're good at feigning human emotions. They're a lot harder to be caught in a crime or even noticed in general because of this," I state.

Everyone's attention is on me, but I don't care. I actually enjoy the classes where I get to study human psychology, and I like boasting about the knowledge Dad has already instilled in me. Knowing human behaviour is a large part of deciding how to take out the target.

The professor smiles at me from the front of the class. "Correct," he says, studying me. "What else can you tell me about them? As you've stated, they're harder to uncover in society, but there have to be certain markers. Right, Miss—" He trails off, waiting for me to give him my name.

"Prescott. And there are. They'll be colder than most individuals in any given situation. They'll always be very self-centred and egotistical, and come across as someone who values their accolades and achievements above anyone else's, say a spouse or children."

"Impressive, Miss Prescott. What else do you know?" he asks, and I shrug.

"A lot, but I don't think that's fair to everyone else. Shouldn't you be giving them a chance to answer?" I ask, making a few of the students chuckle with the professor.

"Very true, Miss Prescott." He turns his eyes back to focus on the class as a whole. "Would anyone like to build on what Miss Prescott just told us?"

I zone out after that, focusing on what homework I have to do when I get back to the dorm.

Dad is supposed to be coming back into the city tomorrow, but I know he's needed elsewhere before I can meet up with him. I want to hear all about his latest hit and pick his brain. It's one of my favourite things to do whenever he gets back from his trips.

When the class is dismissed, I pack my shit up and head for the door, intent on getting something to eat.

"Hey! Hey, hold up!" someone calls from behind me, and I keep going. No one is going to want to talk to me.

"Hey! Are you intentionally ignoring me?" the voice asks again, and I turn to look, curious who they're after.

A guy jogs up to me, smiling wide, and I raise an eyebrow in question. "Can I help you?"

"Hey, thanks for stopping," he says, still grinning like a fool. "For a minute there, I didn't think you were going to."

"Probably because I wasn't," I tell him honestly with a shrug.

He frowns. "Well, why not?"

Oh boy, here we go.

"I didn't figure you were calling out for me." Isn't that obvious? We don't even know each other.

"That's fair, I guess. But I don't know your name,

and I didn't think you'd like me calling you Prescott." He shrugs, the smile back on his face.

"Why not? It's my name. At least then I would have known you were hollering at me," I say. "Why were you hollering at me?"

Obviously, if he knows my last name, he was in the class that just let out, but I still don't get why he wants to talk to me.

"I wanted to tell you how cool it was that you knew some of the stuff back there." He beams at me, clearly flirting. It takes everything not to roll my eyes at him.

If he finds that small show of knowledge impressive enough to flirt, with absolutely no signs of interest given, I don't think we'll have much in common.

Don't get me wrong. It's nice he came up to compliment me, but I've been nothing but formal with him and he's spent the last few minutes smiling at me like he knows he's hot shit. As if that alone is what will have me falling at his feet.

I can tell by his body language that he thinks he's the cream of the crop, and I'm sure that smile disarms a lot of people. I'm just not one of them.

"Thanks," I say, taking a small step back, but his smile only grows before he's moving with me like he's going to walk me wherever I'm going.

"No problem," he states, turning to walk backward as I keep moving. Apparently, he doesn't want to stop facing me. "So, we have this huge party going on at our house tomorrow night. You should totally come."

"I appreciate the offer, but I'm not exactly the party type." It's the truth.

While I enjoy getting together sometimes with a few of the acquaintances I told Melanie about, I'm really not into the whole party scene. I prefer to be aware of everything going on around me at all times, and the loud noise paired with alcohol and drugs just feels like a disaster waiting to happen.

"Your style says otherwise." He smirks at me while checking me out. Suddenly, I don't feel like being so nice anymore.

"Are you aware of just how chauvinistic that sounds?" I practically growl, and he shrugs.

"It's true. Usually, girls dressed like you like to party hard."

I narrow my eyes at him, ready to knock him down a few pegs, when my phone vibrates. Quickly checking my watch, I see Melanie's name and decide I'd much rather talk to her than waste my time on this prick.

"Hey," I greet her the second I pull my phone out and answer it.

"Hey, what are you doing for dinner? Your day is over now, right?" she asks, and I smile. Dickhead looks angry that I dared to answer a call when he was speaking to me, and that gives me immense satisfaction.

"Mine is, but I thought you had a lecture," I state, and the idiot looks agitated.

"I do, but I'm not going. Meet me in the cafeteria?" she asks, and I nod.

"Sure. I'll be there in a few minutes." I hang up, putting my phone back in my pocket.

"That was rude," he states, making me actually laugh.

"So was your insinuation that my clothing choices were directly attached to being a *party girl*." I say the last two words with finger quotations.

He scoffs, shaking his head in clear annoyance. "Whatever, are you coming or not?" he asks, and I smile.

"Not. But thanks for the invite, dude I don't know." Okay, that was probably bitchier than it needed to be, but he pissed me off when I'm hangry. I can't be held accountable for my bitch-meter right now.

"The name is Matt," he says, reaching into his pocket and pulling out a card. "Call me when you change your mind, Prescott. You won't be disappointed." He winks and walks away while I stare after him, completely baffled at how clueless he is.

I look down at the card he handed me, rolling my eyes when I see his name and number on it under the logo for some fraternity. Figures.

Crunching the card up, I push it into my pocket to dispose of later and make my way to the cafeteria to meet up with Melanie.

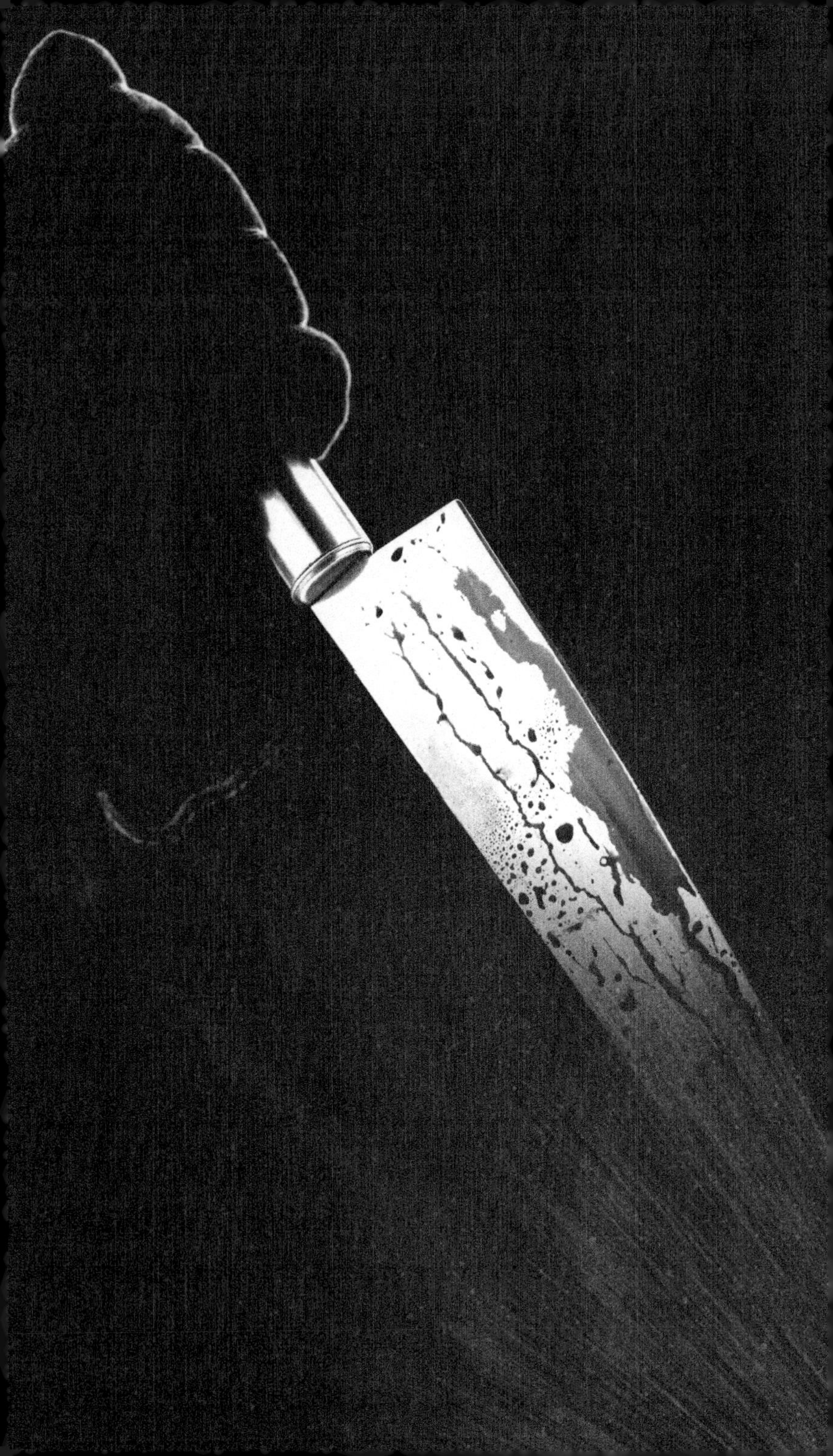

CHAPTER 9
MELANIE

SKIPPING a lecture isn't usually something I do, but I haven't been able to focus today. I keep thinking back to everything Mom always told me about her sisters and trying to connect it to the cold reception I received yesterday. I just can't reconcile the two.

"You look lost in your own world," Daria says, dropping into the chair beside me, snapping me out of my thoughts.

I sigh, giving her a sad smile. "Kind of am, I guess. I decided to go to tomorrow's party for the pledges and tell them I'm not claiming my spot as a legacy," I tell her, feeling more secure in my decision now that I've voiced it aloud.

"You sure?" she questions gently, studying my face.

"I am. The girls I met last night aren't anything

like the ones Mom spoke so highly of. I don't think for a second she would want me to be in a situation that makes me upset or uncomfortable."

"What did they say to make you uncomfortable?" she growls, her eyes narrowed like she's ready to kick someone's ass.

"It doesn't matter, honestly. All that matters is I know before I commit, and I'm able to make the right decision," I explain, letting her know I don't need her to fight my battles for me. Although, her getting upset in my defence is pretty sweet.

"What if you looked into other sororities? Maybe she just wanted you to experience a system of love and support. It doesn't have to be that particular sorority," she says quietly, trying so hard to keep the scowl off her face.

I smile, trying not to laugh at her discomfort. "Truth is, if it wasn't something Mom had loved and wanted for me, I would never have thought of joining." I shrug, reaching over to grip her hand in mine before I can even think.

The second her fingers close around mine, I feel energy zap through my fingers, making me gasp. Lifting my eyes to look at her, I can see the same shock in her eyes, but she doesn't let go.

"Th—that's okay," she says after clearing her throat. "It's okay to be exactly who you want to be.

You're perfect as you are," she whispers with a smirk.

I laugh, pulling my hand from hers before I can make things awkward. "Perfect is a strong word."

"Everyone has their own version of what they think is perfect. You just have to find someone whose idea fits yours. Perfect means something different to everyone." Her words hit me square in the chest, clogging my throat with emotion.

"Oh, fuck," Daria curses.

I move my eyes to where she's looking, and Deedra is walking our way with some guy.

"Well, isn't this a funny coincidence," the guy says, slinging his arm around Deedra's shoulders as she watches us with disdain.

"Matty, come on," she says, turning her entire body away from us, and Daria snorts.

"Yeah, listen to your girlfriend, Matty," she taunts, and my eyes widen.

"Not my girlfriend. Just a cool chick I like to hang with," he says, his eyes not once leaving Daria.

"I think she'd say otherwise. What do you need?" Daria asks, folding her arms across her chest. The guy's eyes drop to her breasts, and I have to hold back the growl rising inside me.

Daria isn't mine. I don't even know for certain

that she likes women, and I barely know her. I need to chill.

He narrows his eyes in annoyance before they flick over to me, almost as an afterthought. Whatever he sees, he doesn't seem to care about because he moves back to Daria, smirking as he squeezes Deedra's ass, making her giggle.

"Are you coming to the party tomorrow night?" he asks Daria without even moving his hand off the redhead's ass. Seriously, this guy is disgusting.

I look at Daria to see how she's going to navigate this situation, but I lean over and whisper into her ear. "Don't cause a scene, okay? She's the one I need to talk to tomorrow night, and I'd prefer her to not be even bitchier."

Daria cuts her eyes to me, a fire brewing in them. She looks calculating and angry, but she nods and reaches over to weave my fingers through hers before turning back to him.

"No, sorry. I already told you I'm not the partying type." She shrugs, gently squeezing my hand where he's looking now with disdain written all over his face. "Besides, I won't be here tomorrow night."

I already know she's planning to go to her dad's place. She plans on bringing things from her parents' places slowly rather than doing what most of us did by bringing it all at once.

I'm not sure whether it's genius or just more work in the long run, but it's her call.

"I think you're making a mistake," he says to her, and I roll my eyes, unable to help myself.

"If she says she's not interested, she's not. Even I couldn't get her to go to pledge night with me." I shrug, squeezing her hand back.

Deedra whips around with a scowl on her face, leering at me before she tenses with one look from Daria.

"Whatever you think you want to say to my girl, Pippy, don't bother." Daria's voice is hard and cold, and it sends a shiver down my spine.

Deedra furrows her brow in confusion. "Who the fuck is Pippy? And whatever, I don't want anything to do with your girlfriend," she sneers, and my heart sinks.

I didn't want Daria to know how others saw me. Call it naïve and delusional, but I wanted her to just keep seeing me the way she has since we met. She's never once been mean or rude to me or treated me like I wasn't good enough.

"Of course you don't get it." Daria rolls her eyes as though she's bored. "But I could tell by your body language that you were about to start spewing some bullshit that no one else cares to hear."

She lets go of my hand, standing up to place both

of her hands on the table, leaning forward in a dark and dominating stance.

"To you, maybe," Deedra snarks, clearly too stupid to sense the threat Daria poses to her right now. Even I take a step back, not recognizing this side of her.

There's clearly a lot I don't know about her, but I hadn't imagined she could look quite this fierce.

"Ask Matty boy, here how good I am at reading body language." She smirks at him as he shifts on his feet, clearly uncomfortable. I just can't tell if he's uncomfortable with the situation as a whole, or with his girlfriend for causing a scene.

"Let's go, Deed," he says, glaring at Daria. "She wants to choose the loser crowd, that's her choice. She'll come crawling to us sooner or later," he says, grabbing Deedra by the arm and pulling her away from the table.

"Wow," I say quietly, feeling the pang of shame in my gut that always accompanies bully confrontations. "I really thought college was going to be better than high school."

Daria turns to me, resting her hands on my shoulders and bending down to look me in the eye. "It will be, Mel. Some people just don't know how to grow up, and it's usually the ones who peak in high school. They try to bully others into feeling bad about themselves so they can continue to feel powerful. Don't give them that power," she says fiercely, squeezing my shoulders in support.

"How are you so unaffected by it?" I ask, wondering how she can be strong enough to not let words affect her.

She smirks, standing up and letting me go. "I have a pretty kick-ass dad who taught me early on that people will always try to bring others down when they're insecure about themselves." She shrugs, looking around the room. "He and Mom always made sure I was confident in who I am. That way, no one could ever bring me down. Come on, let's go get some pizza. I'd rather eat in our room," she says, and I breathe out in relief.

"You're pretty lucky to be that confident in yourself. And pizza sounds perfect."

It's not until I'm lying in bed later in the night that I realize she never corrected them about my being her girlfriend.

I fall asleep with a smile on my face, knowing that I may have found the connection with Daria that Mom always talked about with the sisterhood.

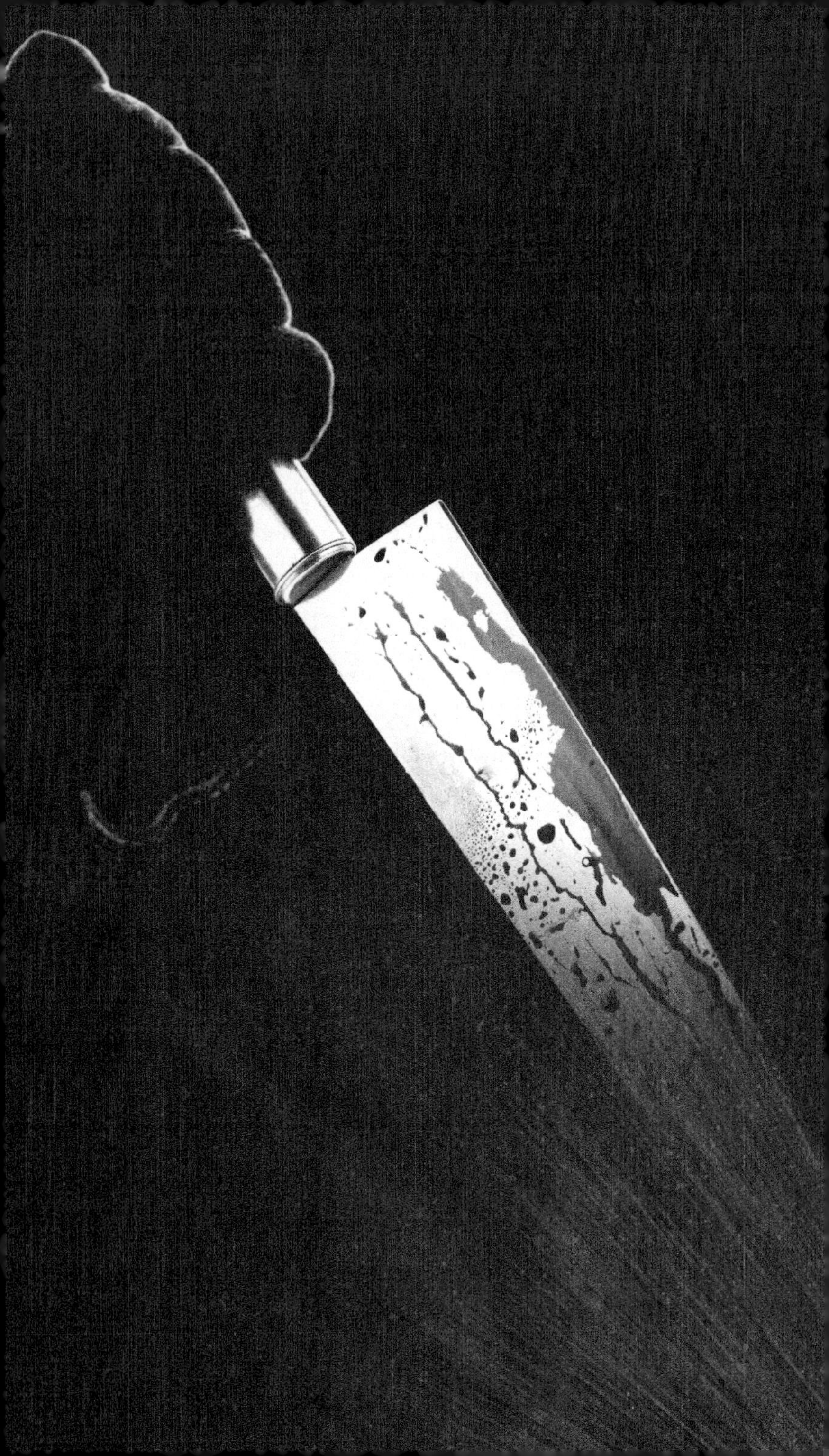

CHAPTER 10
DARIA

"You sure you want to be there? It's not too late for me to come back and hang out. I can grab my shit another night," I tell Mel over the phone, knowing she's been nervous about this all day.

"No, it's okay. Hey, maybe you'll get lucky and your dad will be home. You said he's back from his business trip, right?" she asks quietly, and I smile.

"He is, yeah. I don't think he's home, though. He has this terrible habit of working so late he ends up sleeping at the office." It's another half-truth. He does work late, but it's very rarely for his legitimate business. He hires other people to pull those long hours.

"Workaholic?" she asks, trying to distract herself from the fact she's almost to the sorority house.

"Workaholic is how some might see it." I laugh,

smiling as I think of how Dad words it. "But he prefers to describe it as him being an active member of society, providing jobs for others in order to help as many families as he can and saving the world with one invention at a time." And actively ridding it of the dark and despicable filth that run rampant around us—but I can't actually say that to her.

"Man is a wordsmith, huh?" she says with a chuckle before sucking in a breath. "I'm here. I'll see you when you get back to the room tonight, okay?"

"Call me if you need me. I don't mind kicking some rude bitch's ass if need be." I smirk, stopping in my tracks when I hear footsteps behind me. "Good luck, babe." I hang up the phone and pocket it, sliding my other hand into my bra to grab for my knife as I start to move again.

Nothing sounds off around me for a moment, and I wonder if I'm just being paranoid when the footsteps sound again. They're light, almost like they're trying not to be heard as we continue walking. If they're after me, I know exactly where they plan on cornering me, and it's right down the street.

By the time I get to the alley and walk into it, I'm already dreading what Dad's going to say if he finds out about this because I didn't take the goddamn car.

"Hey, baby, where you headed all alone?" one of

them says behind me, and I roll my eyes. How fucking unoriginal.

I ignore them and pick up my speed a little, acting like any woman would when she's alone in a relatively dark alleyway. Maybe I'll just run them in circles until I get bored and lose them. It would be easier than confrontation.

"Don't run. I won't hurt you," he says, taunting me.

"Please, I need to get to my dad's," I say in a higher voice, showing fear I do not feel.

A hand grabs at my hair, yanking me back so hard I actually yelp. Fuck, that hurt. Why do they always go for the fucking hair?!

"Ouch!" I cry out, tears unwillingly coming to my eyes from the sharp sting in my scalp.

"You're being a rude little bitch," another one spits out. He moves ahead of us and bends down, his face covered in a ski mask. "We were warned you would be, though."

Warned? By fucking who? It's not like anyone knows who the fuck I am in regards to Dad, so this can't be about him. And even if it were, would they really know I was a bitch by default?

"Wh—what?" I stutter when the asshole yanks on my hair again. I hiss, grinding my teeth through the pain. "I don't understand what you're talking about," I tell them as a third guy makes himself present.

Three is about what I assumed based on the rhythm of their footsteps, but I'll hold out another few minutes to see exactly what I'm dealing with before knowing how to attack.

"Are we going to play with her first?" the newest one asks, sounding almost bored, and I try my best to keep the sneer off of my face. Good fucking luck with that, asshole.

"Matt said we could, as long as we made sure to have her there for the main event," the one behind me, gripping my hair, says.

Matt. Oh, he's going to pay dearly for whatever the fuck this is. And what main event? I told that bastard I wasn't going to his party. Jesus, dude needs to take the hint.

"I wouldn't if I were you," I say under my breath.

"What was that, Prescott?" the guy yanks my hair again.

I take a deep breath to calm myself. "Please don't. I don't know why he's so angry," I say a little louder. "I just told him I wasn't interested."

One of the guys in front of me snorts. "You don't say no to a man like Matthew Simcoe without some form of consequences."

Really? Did he actually just say that? The way some people think so highly of themselves is gross.

"So, what you're telling me is he's a spoiled brat with control issues," I state, rolling my eyes.

I'm getting more comfortable knowing there are only three of them. I think if there were any more, they would have made themselves known by now.

"And you pissed him off. Lucky you," the third one drawls.

"Look, you don't want to hurt me. His issues aren't worth you going to jail over," I tell them, moving my hands to my chest in a show of fear for them, and they don't think twice about it.

Why would they? According to their intel, I'm just some little bitch that turned their friend down, and now he wants payback.

"No one is going to jail because you won't remember any of this," the one behind me says. It's that moment when the corner of my eye catches onto a needle coming at me, and I'm done.

"Wrong move, asshole," I grind out. I twirl my body from his grasp, twisting my hair with the hold he has on me.

Once I've maneuvered away from the needle that barely pricked me, I reach into my bra and pull my knife out. Flicking it open, I quickly swing it at the arm attached to the hand in my hair.

He lets out a scream, releasing my hair quickly. I stand up, taking in where the other two are, and seeing if he still has a hold on the needle. He does.

I move fast, ducking under his bleeding arm before swiping the knife at his other hand, until he drops the syringe with another cry of pain.

"You cunt!" he screams, before barking at the other two. "Fucking grab her! Don't just stand there!"

They lunge for me, and I dive for the syringe to break it, but one grabs me around the waist. When he reaches for my arms, I twist and stab the knife into his side, breaking free when his hold loosens.

"Fuck!" he hisses, bending over while he holds his waist.

"Put the knife down, kitten." It comes from the guy that seemed to be bored with everything until now. "I don't want to hurt you," he tells me, and I laugh.

"Liar."

He smirks at my attitude while bending down to grab the needle. "Fine. I don't want to make you bleed. I'd rather have you looking so beautiful while you're tied up, taking my dick."

"Sorry, I'm a lesbian. You don't do it for me," I drawl, moving in a small circle, readying for his attack while listening for the other two.

"You're only a lesbian because you haven't had the right dick yet." He shrugs like it's a known fact, but before I can chew him out for being a crass, uneducated prick, I hear one of the others running toward me.

I swing around, stabbing where I know their gut will be. Now he's bleeding from both of his arms and his stomach. Moron.

Taking my eyes off the one with the drugs costs me. He wraps his one arm around my throat, instantly cutting my air off while the one with the side wound grabs my arms and takes the knife from me.

"Now, now, kitten. That wasn't very nice of you," he hisses into my ear as he moves the needle to my hip. Rookie fucking mistake, but I almost miss it from the lack of oxygen.

I close my eyes and remember my training, even through the fog. I drop my weight, and he grunts, letting me fall to the ground as I gasp for air.

I swing my leg to knock him down, before scrambling to grab his hand and force the needle—that he's still holding onto—into his neck, using his own fingers to plunge the drugs into his system.

The other one comes at me from behind, and I twirl on him, knocking his feet out from under him before pulling the knife out of my boot and stabbing him in the chest. Play time is fucking over.

"You'll pay for this," the drugged one says, slurring his words.

"So will you," I tell him, breathing heavily as I fall to the ground on my knees.

I crawl toward the asshole who isn't drugged. He's already pale and lying on the ground in a pool of blood, but I look into his eyes as I drive the knife into his chest.

"Pl—" he tries to speak, but he's lost too much strength. I know he won't get back up.

Crawling back to the last guy, he's already passed out when I shove the knife into his chest and collapse onto my back, energy draining from me as the sounds of the city filter down the alley in the sudden quiet.

When I've mustered the energy to move, I wipe my bloodied hands on my jeans, then pull my phone out to dial the one person I know can make this go away.

He's going to be fucking pissed.

"Daria?" he says into the phone, his voice calming me, and I sigh.

"Dad, I need your help." My voice shakes as another round of exhaustion hits me. Apparently, killing three men isn't as easy as I'd thought. Good to know.

"Are you safe? Where are you?" he barks down the line.

After rattling off the address and promising him I'm safe, I let the phone fall to my side before my eyes droop.

Fuck. Maybe they got some of the drugs into me after all…

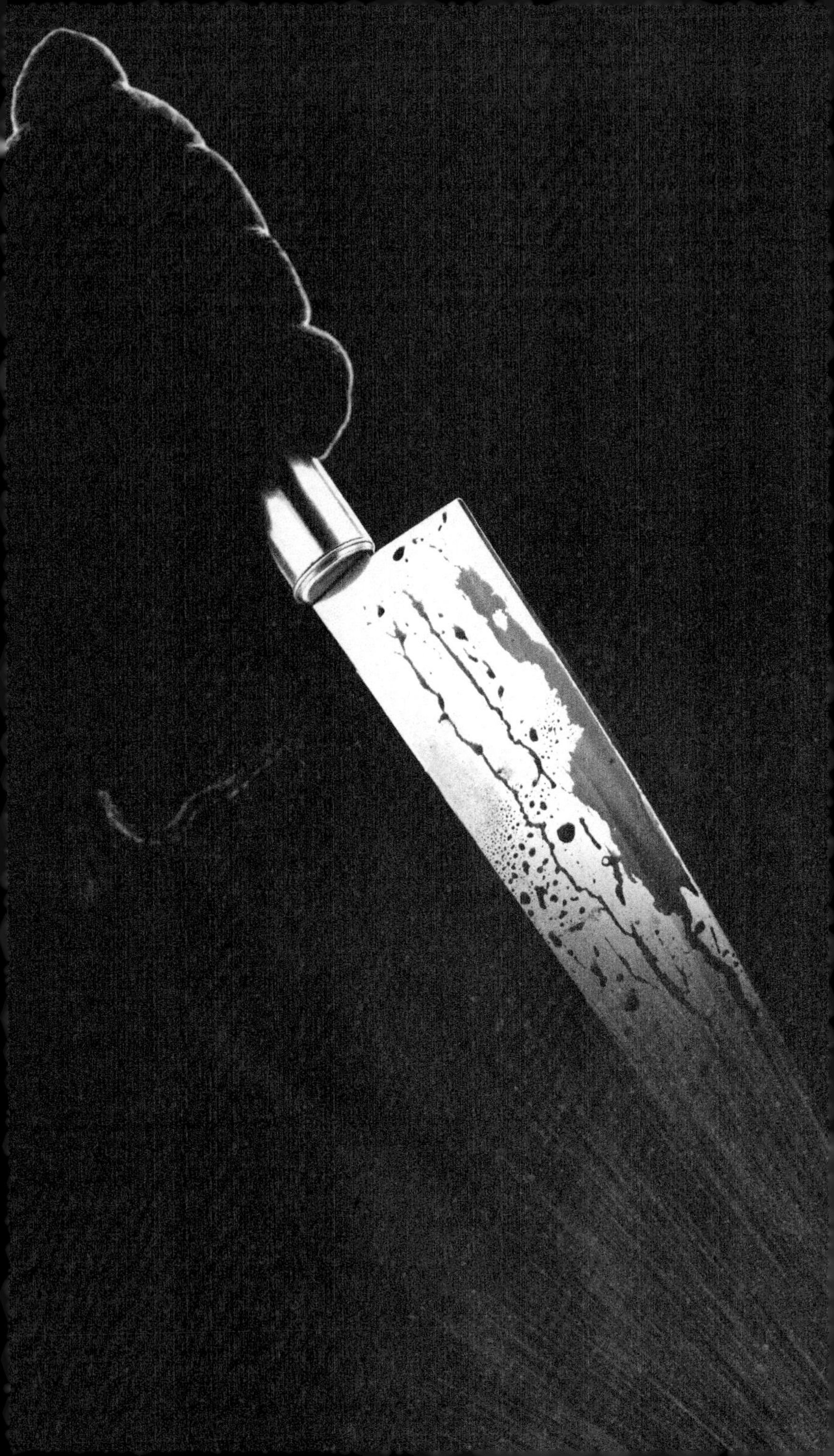

CHAPTER 11
DARIA

"It looks like she was stuck in the neck," I hear someone say. I think it's Carlos.

"I'll kill whoever is responsible for this," Dad growls, his hand brushing my hair, and I sigh.

"Daddy," I whisper, feeling lethargic.

"Thank Christ, Daria," Dad lets out a strangled breath.

"How long was I out?" I question, trying to sit up, but he doesn't let me.

"Twenty minutes, maybe less," he says to me quietly. "Carlos thinks they got you with some of whatever the fuck was in that syringe."

I wince. "I didn't even feel it dig in. Thought I avoided it," I tell him honestly.

We start moving, and I realize Dad has me in the SUV already.

"You did amazing, sweetheart. I'm so fucking proud of you," he praises me, but I know it won't last. "That being said, what the fuck were you doing in an alley by yourself? Where is the car?" he asks, his tone hard.

"Dad," I groan, forcing myself to sit up.

"No. Don't you dare 'Dad' me right now, Daria Elizabeth Prescott. You were attacked!"

"I'm fine."

His growl is so loud I even see Carlos wince.

"The fact that I have a cleaning crew disposing of three bodies and all physical evidence of a crime right now says otherwise, kid."

"I know, I know." I shake my head, annoyed by what happened. "Sorry," I mumble.

I'm trying to work everything out in my head now that I'm awake and in the car, but it doesn't make any sense that things went that far. I wasn't about to let them rape me, though, and they weren't taking no for an answer. I probably should have just knocked them out, but justice wouldn't have been served that way. How many others have they raped in the past and gotten away with it?

"They weren't anyone I recognize," he says after a moment, watching me closely.

"Yeah, I knew it didn't have to do with your

work," I tell him, looking out the window as their words continue to run through my mind.

What was the main event they were supposed to take me to?

"You knew?"

"Yeah," I sigh, turning to look at him. "I pissed some asshole frat guy off at school, and this was some form of retaliation."

His face thunders with darkness. "Since when do little asshole shits try to grab a woman off the streets?" he hisses. "Don't answer that. I've killed pricks like them before."

I swallow the anxiousness down as I look into his eyes, knowing he's going to lose his shit.

"They weren't meant to kill me. They wanted to rape me before taking me to some event that the asshole has going on..." I trail off, my mind running a million miles a minute.

"I'm glad their de—"

"Carlos! Get to sorority row. NOW!" I yell, realizing there's one thing Matt and tonight have in common.

It's fucking pledge night, and Melanie is there with them. It wouldn't surprise me if they tried to hurt her, and I need to stop it.

If I'm not already too late after passing out.

Fuck.

"Why are we here?" Dad asks me, taking in the rigidness of my posture.

"Melanie," I tell him, getting out of the car and running for the *Beta Delta Phi* house.

He stays in the car, just like I knew he would, but I know I'm not alone. Carlos is right on my heels as I run into the house in search of my roommate and friend.

I have this feeling in the pit of my stomach, and it's never wrong. I wasn't the only one they were after tonight.

"Where is Deedra?" I bark at one of the other girls, grabbing her arm roughly.

She shakes beneath my hold, but I refuse to feel bad about it. "I—I don't know! Her and a few of the other girls left a little while ago," she whimpers, and my panic starts to surface.

"Where? Where did they go?!" I snap, giving her a little shake.

"I really don't know. They left with Matt and a few of the others," she tells me, pleading with her eyes for me to let her go.

"Do you know where they could have gone?" I ask, letting up on her arm a little.

She sniffles, shaking her head. "Maybe the basement at the Kappa house? They go there to party someti—" I let her go and run back out of the house.

"What's going on, Dar?" Carlos asks me, jogging to keep up as I run across the street.

"The leader of this frat sent those guys to rape me, Carlos," I rasp, refusing to let my fear take hold. "They said they would have fun with me before the main event. I may have pissed him off, but his girlfriend is a massive bitch toward Melanie. What if I'm not the only main event?" I ask, refusing to slow down as I storm through their front door.

"Fuck!" Carlos curses as I run right into Matt.

"I see you came to the party after all," Matt snarks, smirking down at me like he doesn't know what he did. Or tried to do to me.

"Where's Melanie?" I ask, moving to stand right against his chest, but he shrugs.

"At home, I presume. After she left here, I really didn't care where she went," he says like he's bored of this conversation already. It's pretty clear he doesn't care.

Maybe he doesn't, but a couple of his housemates look a little uneasy behind him as they watch our interaction. Something happened. I just don't know what.

Moving more into his space, knowing Carlos will help me out if I need it—and with the bit of drugs in my system, I just might—I stand on my toes and get right in his face.

"If she's hurt in any way, so help me, I will bury you," I hiss.

He looks smug until my words sink in, his eyes widening just a bit. I don't think he's used to being threatened in such a deadly tone. Good.

I move away from him and head back to the car, not waiting for him to respond. I need to get back to the dorms. Now.

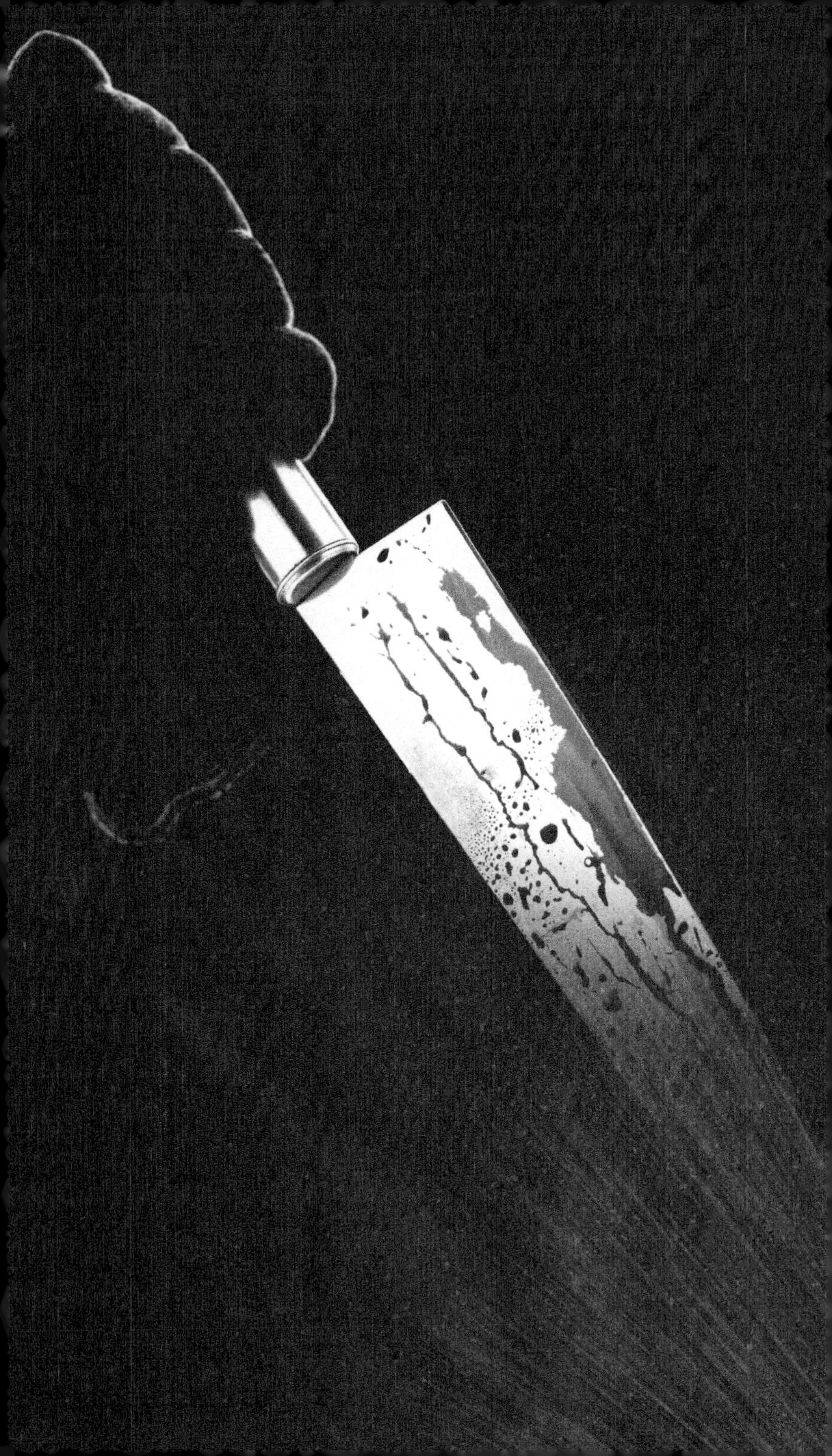

CHAPTER 12
MELANIE

"Mel? Mel!"

Someone is calling my name, probably Daria, but I can't answer her.

As the voice gets closer and sharper, I let out an involuntary cry.

No, no, no, no. Stay away, please! Don't touch me. Don't come near me. She can't come near me.

"Melanie!" she gasps when she enters the bathroom and sees me sitting on the shower floor fully dressed.

Wash it off. Wash it all off.

"Hey, Melanie, it's me. It's Daria. Can you hear me?" she asks, getting closer.

I cry, throwing myself back away from her touch.

"NO!" God, please don't touch me.

Walk away. Just walk away.

"I'm not walking away from you, baby. Whatever happened, I'm here," she says gently, moving slower and stepping into the shower with me, but on the other end.

She's getting wet. So wet.

"Don't care. This isn't the first time I've sat in a shower with clothes on." She looks at the door before looking back at me, but I don't move my eyes off the bottom of the tub. "Mind you, those were to sober my friends up before my parents found out. They really don't like people who are irresponsible being around me," she whispers, snorting.

A part of me wonders why she's whispering that, but I just can't. I can't process any of it.

Cold. Dirty. Whore.

"No, no, no," I whisper, rocking back and forth as I start clawing at my clothes. "Off. Get it off." I rip and pull at them until my hands hurt, but I can't lift them over my head. I can't move.

"You need your clothes off?" she asks me gently, moving a little closer to me.

I whimper, wrapping my arms around me and slam my eyes shut. "Dirty. Burn. No." It's all I can say.

I feel so fucking broken right now, like there's just a shell where I existed earlier tonight.

"Mel, no," Daria growls at me. "I don't know

exactly what's happened, but I can take a guess, and right now I know there's not much I can do to tell you that your thoughts are wrong. But listen to me." She moves closer, a little at a time, and I feel the tears running down my face.

"No, please," I beg, trying to back away from her. It's not that I want her to keep her distance, but she won't see me the same way anymore.

I'm tainted and unclean. Used.

"Melanie, please stop being afraid of me," she begs, and I wish I could stop it.

"Clothes," I rasp, pulling at them and refusing to make eye contact with her. "Need to burn." I swallow down the bile rising at the images that come flooding back as I rip at my clothes.

"Okay, okay. Will you let me help you out of them?" she asks.

She reaches her hand out to gently lift my chin with her finger, and the concern I see in her eyes breaks what little composure I was pretending to hold on to.

"Please," I whisper, my voice cracking. "Make it stop."

"I'll do my best. You want to start with tossing these clothes and cleaning up?" she asks, and I nod. Unable to say anything. "Can I touch you right now?

Just to help," she hedges, and I close my eyes tight, my whole body shaking.

"Y—yes," I croak out, and she nods her head.

"I'm going to need you to keep your pretty eyes on me, alright? Don't close them while we're doing this. I need your mind to stay present, so you know who is touching you at all times. Can you do that for me, Mel?"

God, I hope so. I nod, letting the tears continue to silently fall.

It takes way longer than I'd like to admit to get the clothes off, and my body clean. Or where I feel clean enough to exist for the moment. When someone knocks on the bathroom door, my entire body freezes to the point of pain.

Who? No, they wouldn't come back. Would they? Daria would lock the door. She's anal about that. Right? Oh, God.

"Shh, it's okay," Daria whispers in my ear as she continues to wrap towels around my head and body. "It's my Dad. Something," she sighs, shaking her head. "Something happened tonight with me, and he had to come get me. I was with him when I realized what was happening."

My heart stops beating as fear takes over every

fibre of my being. Her dad? Something happened to her?

I can't process any of it through the fear.

"Daria?" a strong male voice sounds from outside the bathroom.

I let out an involuntary whimper as my body begins to tremble.

"Hey, Dad, can you grab the pair of pyjamas off of Melanie's bed, please? And bring me something of mine to wear," she says loud enough for him to hear her through the door.

"Of course. Is everything alright?" he asks, and she watches me closely as she responds.

"Not really, but it will be. We just need to get dressed first, then I need to talk to you."

"Okay, sweetheart. Be right back." It only takes him a minute before he's telling us the clothes are outside of the door.

"Thanks, Dad. I'll be right out," she says before turning back to me. "I'm going to go grab the clothes and quickly change into some dry ones. Do you want some privacy to get dressed?"

She's being so gentle with me right now, and I don't know how to feel. A part of me feels like a useless piece of garbage for allowing myself to shut down like this. To need so much help that I've become a burden to her.

The other part of me is too numb. All I want to do is stare off into nothingness and forget the world, but I answer her the only way I know I can.

"Please," I whisper, knowing I can't stand anyone else's eyes on my naked body again. Not even hers.

"Okay. Give me a sec to change out of mine. I can do it in the corner out of your eyesight if that helps." She goes to the door and opens it just enough to pull in the clothes her father set out and gets to work on quickly changing out of my direct line of sight. Just like she said she would.

Once she exits, I stare at the closed door for long moments, knowing I really don't deserve someone like her right now.

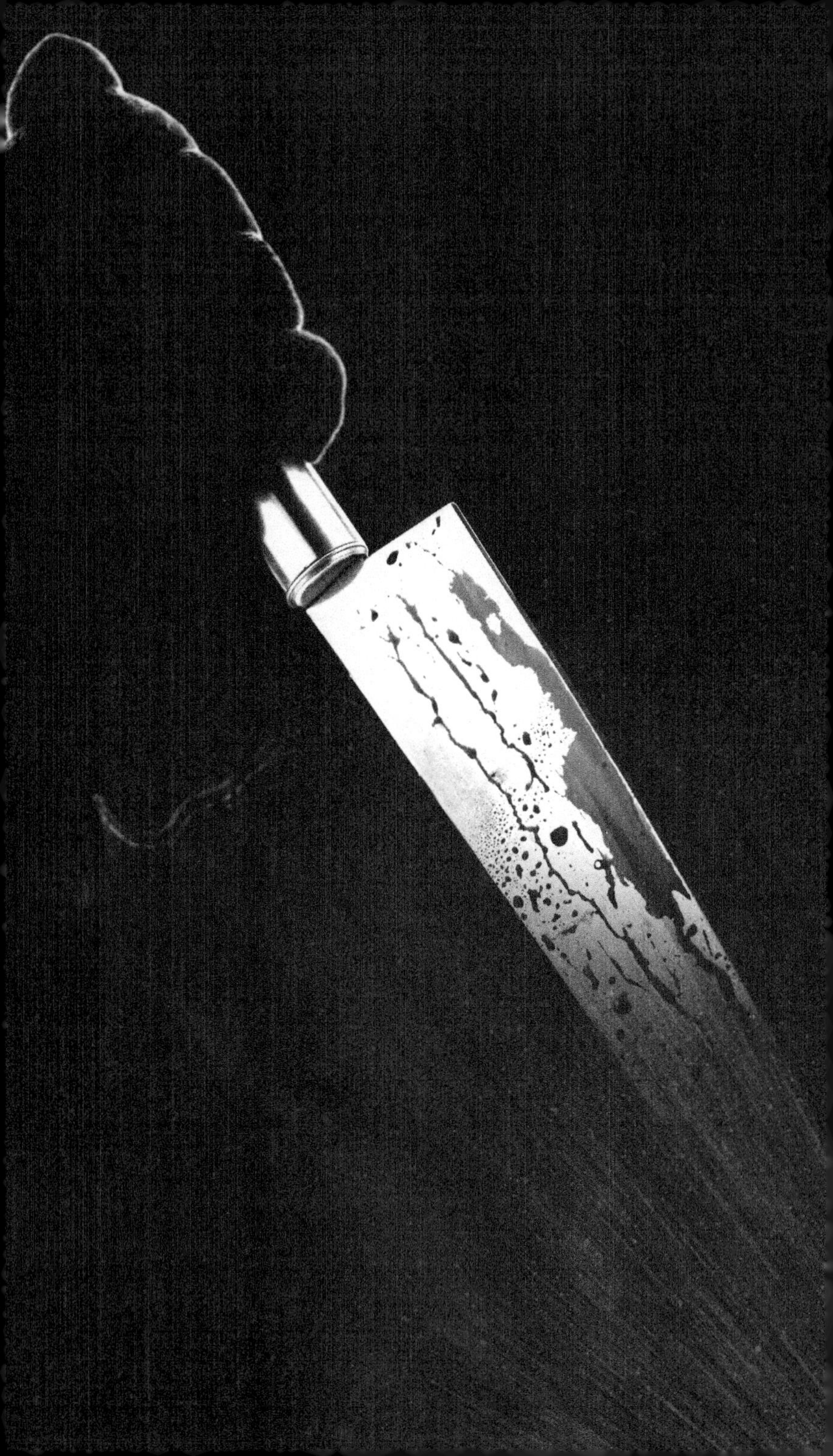

CHAPTER 13
DARIA

Concern covers Dad's face when I make my way into the other room, leaving Melanie alone to get dressed.

God, they raped her. I know they did. She wouldn't react this way otherwise, and that knowledge fucking infuriates me. I wish I could bring the other bastards back so I can kill them slower for even trying to take part in anything that has happened tonight.

"What happened?" Dad asks quietly when I sit down beside him.

"Let's just say she isn't the same girl I left when I headed to your apartment," I growl out, balling my fists on my thighs. "They did to her what the others failed to do to me."

"Fucking Christ!" he barks, then winces at the

harshness of it. "Why would they hurt her if this is about you?" he asks, turning to me.

I swallow back the anger and raw emotion clogging my throat, refusing to let them control me right now. I can't be a normal friend tonight. I need to be the killer's daughter.

"The guy I pissed off?" I start, and he nods with a frown. "His girlfriend is the head of the sorority Mel is a legacy at," I explain, and he continues to frown.

"And that means anything, why?" he questions, and I understand his confusion. What Deedra and Matt have headed up tonight is purely malicious.

"You remember the movie *Mean Girls* that I was obsessed with when I was younger?"

"How could I forget that goddamn thing? I still know that you're supposed to wear pink on Wednesdays. Do you know how emasculating that is?" he asks, his lips twitching with the threat of a smile.

Despite everything that's happened tonight, I chuckle.

"Deedra is like Regina George, the top mean girl in the movie by the way, on steroids." I sigh. "I don't know a lot of what happened with them, but it was pretty clear that she didn't like Melanie."

"I still don't understand how that leads to them raping you both," he hisses, and I shrug.

"Does it have to be logical? I know why Matt

would want to hurt me. I bruised his ego by turning him down, and he didn't like it." I shake my head, still confused how Melanie became a part of this whole thing.

"They wanted to scare me," Melanie rasps from the door of the bathroom.

Dad's body locks up, looking uncomfortable that he's been seen by someone, so I take his hand in mine. When he turns to look at me, I smile.

"It's okay, Dad. She won't tell anyone," I tell him.

Melanie slowly walks over to her bed before pulling all of her blankets off the bed and wrapping them around herself.

"What?" she asks, looking between Dad and me, her stare blank.

"Mel, I know you're in a state of shock, but I need you to promise you won't tell anyone who my dad is. He doesn't want the world knowing he has a daughter," I say quietly.

"Don't say it like that, Daria. Christ, she's going to think I'm ashamed of you," he groans, shaking his head before focusing on my friend.

"Sorry," I wince, not realizing just how the way I worded it could come across. I've never had to explain my relationship with my him to anyone before because no one has ever met him, so this is all new territory for both of us.

"What she means is, I am a very powerful man in the tech industry, and I've made a lot of enemies over the years." He clears his throat, looking uncomfortable. "I don't want the world to know she's my daughter because there's a chance that someone could use her against me," he explains, and Mel just blinks at him.

"K," she whispers, closing her eyes. She looks fucking exhausted, and I hate that for her.

"You said they wanted to scare you?" I ask gently, wondering what that means.

She whimpers and tightens the blankets around her even more. "Didn't want me to change my mind about pledging."

"That doesn't make sense why all of this has happened tonight," I muse out loud, trying to find a connection.

"He's mad at you," she whispers. "Said things about…" She trails off, shaking her head as the tears begin to fall.

"It's okay, Mel. You don't have to talk right now." I get up and move over to her bed, being sure to move slowly.

"I—I have to—get it—out," she says between sobs.

"Okay, okay. Then I'm listening," I whisper, and wait her out.

Dad watches us in silence while I comfort her the best I know how. He's going to warn me about getting attached to others, but he'll always support my decisions no matter what.

"He said… he said he was going to teach you a lesson," she says between sobs, her eyes fused shut as she tells the story. "That—that you can't just say no to him, then flaunt our relationship in front of him like he's nothing." She shakes and tightens the blanket even more, and my anger grows.

"Relationship?" Dad asks, and I look at him.

"There's something here. What he'd be referring to is when I told him off while holding Mel's hand yesterday," I explain.

"Jesus, Daria," Dad groans. "I thought you were trying to keep a low profile here."

I raise an eyebrow at him. "He insinuated I'd be up to party and sleep with him because of how I dress."

His eyes darken. "Never mind, I take it back. He deserves worse," he growls, and I know he wants to kill Matt. He wanted to for the attack in the alley tonight, but now it's even worse.

"I'll handle it," I tell him darkly, making Melanie jump.

"Without describing what he did, because I refuse

to put you through that, can you tell me what else happened?" I ask her, and she nods.

"They watched," she croaks. "Deedra a—and six of their friends." She takes a deep, shuddering breath. "They—he wanted to hurt you while making me watch," she cries, shaking her head.

"Bastard," I growl, and she cries harder.

"He was waiting for you, but you didn't come. I don't—I don't know why he thought you would."

"Daria was… attacked tonight," Dad says carefully, making Mel gasp, her eyes wide and full of fear.

"No!" she cried, and I wish I could stab Dad just a little right now for worrying her.

"I'm fine. I promise you, Mel. I'm alright. Dad taught me how to be a badass, and I got away," I tell her, fibbing a little.

"Why did they do all of this? How can people be so evil?" she asks, and I shrug.

"There's a lot of evil in this world, Mel. I just really wish you hadn't seen it."

I don't know how Melanie will handle what's happened to her as the days go on, but her being raped is my fault. If I had just allowed them to take me, I could have saved her the way I'd saved myself.

"You couldn't have known, Daria," Dad says quietly.

I turn to look at him. He can see the need for revenge and bloodshed on my face and nods. He'll give this to me. He'll do whatever I need him to in order to rid the world of Melanie's nightmares.

Not for her, but for me. Because he knows they intended to harm me, and he won't allow them to live for that reason. Also because he can see Mel means something to me, and he knows I won't let anyone live who harms those I care about.

Matt and Deedra, your days are numbered. I'm coming for you.

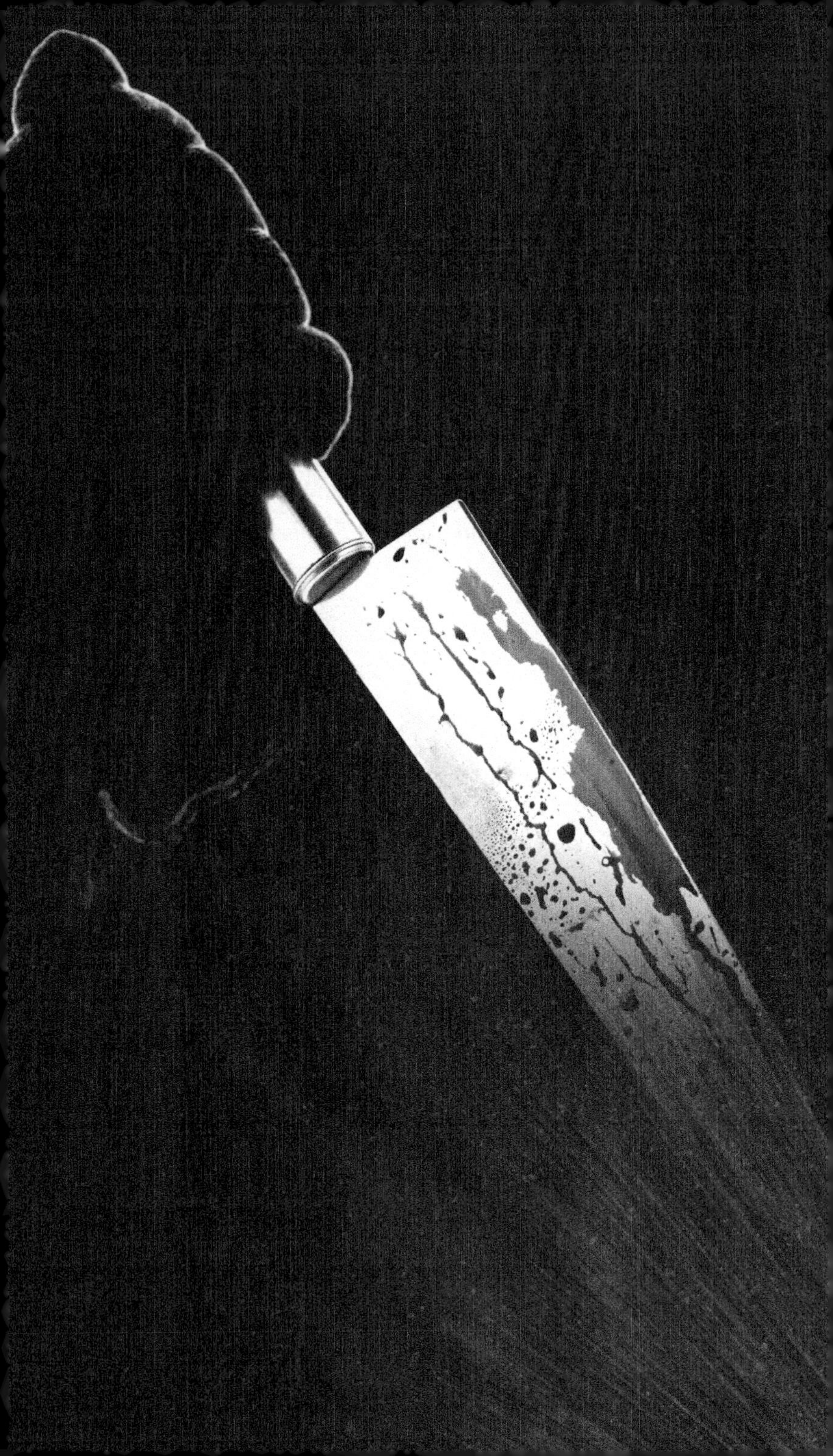

CHAPTER 14
MELANIE

Two days.

That's how long it's been since my life was altered forever. The day I realized there are darker things in this world than cancer.

I always knew that people like that existed, I just never imagined I would experience it firsthand. How two people could be so cruel and demeaning is absolutely horrifying. So is the fact that about six others watched it all happen and did absolutely nothing to stop them.

I had an entire audience to witness the destruction of who I was before. They watched as Deedra held me down, and Matt took away my choice. They just stood there, witnessing as the two of them worked together to rape me, taking away my choice, my self respect, and my dignity all in one go.

Aside from the small amounts of food and water I've been able to keep down, I have spent the last two days sleeping. It's easier to sleep and ignore the pain in my heart from everything that happened, even with the nightmares. At least in my dreams I can pretend it's not real.

After the shower and talk in our dorm, Daria's dad insisted on letting us stay in his penthouse apartment, stating he wanted to keep an eye on us. Well, Daria. I don't think he'd give me a second glance if Daria didn't insist on staying by my side.

Sighing, I force myself out of bed to have a shower.

The hot water feels good on my skin, but I'm instantly transported back to myself paralyzed in the shower at our dorm. I turn the water up as hot as I can stand it and start scrubbing at my skin, feeling raw and open.

I want to erase the feel of their hands from my body. If I could bathe in a tub of straight bleach, I would, but I don't think it would help. It's like their touch is seared into every place they touched.

When I can't handle it anymore, I open the shower door and run to the toilet, dry heaving as I start to cry, my entire body shaking.

When will this stop? I don't want to play their victim. I hate feeling so worthless and used.

Once the nausea has passed, I stand on shaky legs to shut the shower off and start drying my body. Cleaning up the water on the floor, I brush my teeth and stare at myself in the mirror, not recognizing the woman looking back at me.

"I can't do this," I whisper to her as tears pool in my eyes. "I can't keep hiding away from the world like I'm not strong enough to push past this."

She stares back at me with a look of pity that infuriates a piece inside of myself. The piece that doesn't want to be her. But that won't change if I don't get my ass out of the bedroom and try to face life.

I throw my wet hair into a ponytail after brushing it, then toss on a clean t-shirt and shorts before taking a deep breath and quietly opening the door.

"You either need to tell her the truth or let her go, Daria," I hear Kane tell her, and I frown.

What is he talking about? Are they talking about me?

"Dad, I can't just come out and tell her the truth," Daria huffs, making my lips quirk a bit. She has a hot temper with her father, and it's something he seems both extremely irritated by and proud of all at the same time.

I've realized through the small interactions I've witnessed these past couple of days that she wasn't fully truthful about his involvement in her life, but I get it.

Kane Fitzpatrick is a legend across the world for his innovations in technology. I'm not even into that shit, and I still know who he is, so it makes sense why Daria has held that secret close to the vest.

The fact she even told me who he was at all after only knowing each other for a week is astounding. Then again, they found me in the worst shape possible, so it's not like they could hide it from me. Not when Daria insisted on being by my side.

"Our lives aren't made for innocents like her, sweetheart. You know this," he reminds her, his voice so gentle it's jarring.

Kane is a huge man. He's easily six-foot-five and built like a linebacker, towering over Daria and essentially the entire population, and the hardness in his eyes is terrifying. They only seem to soften when they land on his daughter, my new best friend.

I move toward their voices, making sure my footsteps land heavy so they can hear me coming.

"Do it, Daria, or let her go," he says once more, quieter as I walk around the corner into the living room.

"I'm sorry," I say, feeling all sorts of confused. "I wasn't meaning to overhear anything, but what…

what are you supposed to tell me?" I ask, my voice quiet and unsure.

Kane narrows his eyes at me as though he's assessing if I can be trusted or not, and I'm not going to lie. His eyes seem even colder than I remember seeing them a few days ago.

"Dad," Daria hisses, pulling his attention back to her. "You're freaking her out. Stop it!"

I chuckle nervously, wringing my hands together as I sit down on a chair across from them. "I'm f—fine," I stammer, and mentally curse myself out.

Kane scoffs, but I see his lips twitch a little in amusement. "Sure you are."

"How are you feeling, Mel?" Daria asks me.

She's looking at me with concern and worry, but not pity, and I thank God for that because I can't even bring myself to look at myself in the mirror without feeling pity for the quiet mouse I've seemed to become.

"Honestly? I don't know. Pissed off, pathetic, exhausted," I tell her, sighing.

"Pissed and exhausted is fine, but don't you dare for one second think that you're pathetic because of that motherfucking bastard." She looks fierce as she spits the words out, and I want to cry.

I'd give anything to take those words and wrap

them around me like a warm blanket, but I can't. I'm just not in a place where I can believe it.

"It's not because of him," I whisper, casting my eyes to the floor.

"Then why?" she asks, getting up and walking over to kneel in front of me before taking my hands in hers.

I let a few tears fall, still unable to look her in the eye, but I focus on our hands fused together in my lap and take a deep breath to ready myself.

"Because... I—I gave up. I quit fighting after the first thrust," I choke on the words. "It was like... the instant he pushed inside of me, I lost my will to live and fight." I lift my eyes to hers as the tears stream down my face, and all I see is a darkness I've never experienced.

She's so angry she's almost feral. Like a wild animal about to strike, and I know it's not aimed at me, but it eases something inside of me all the same.

God, I'm freaking broken to feel that way, but in this moment, all I wish is that she could rid the world of their presence so I can breathe again.

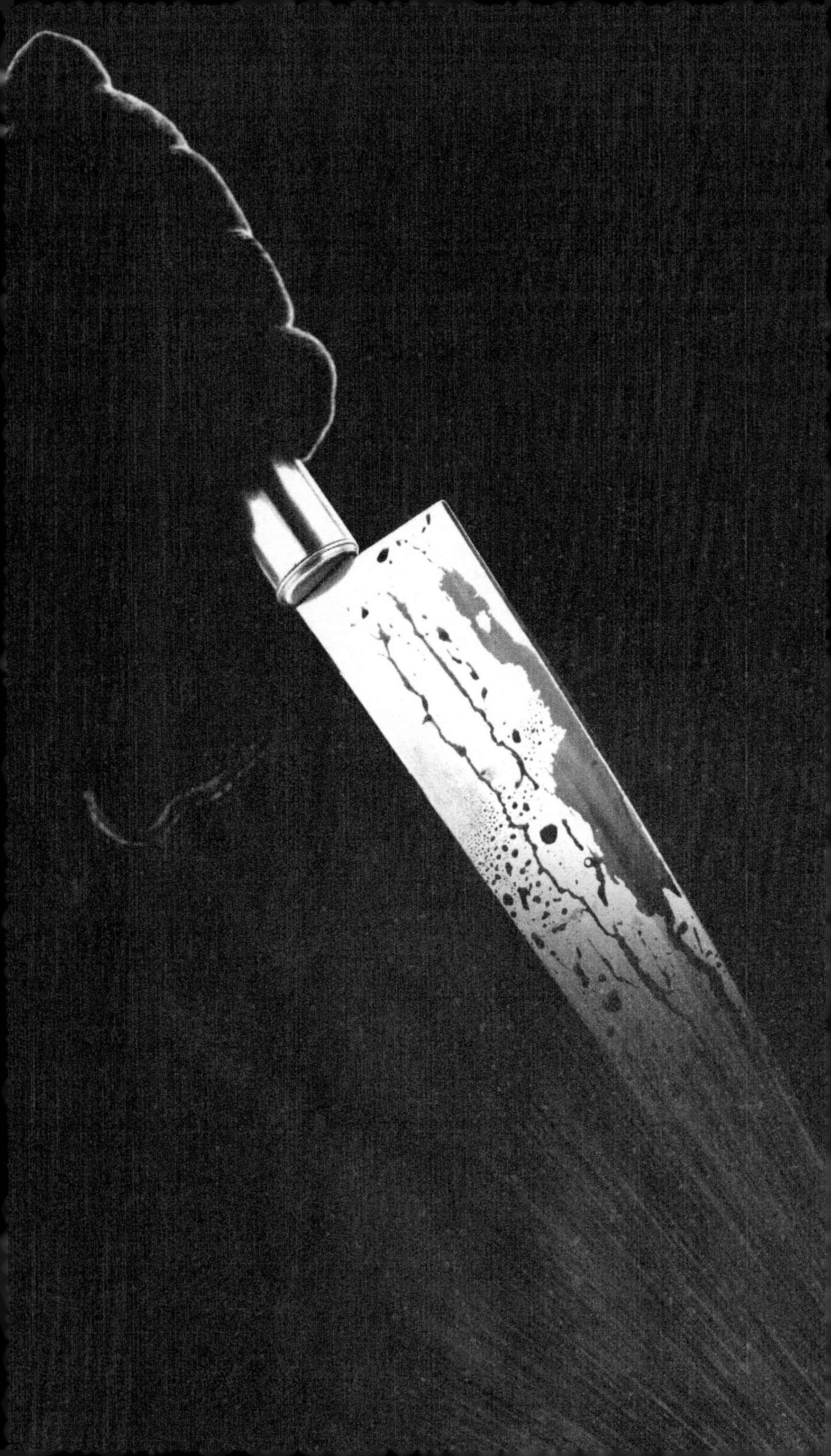

CHAPTER 15
DARIA

Murder.

That's the only thing running through my mind right now. If those three bastards that attacked me deserved to die, then Matthew and Deedra deserve to be tortured until they take their very last breaths. And I'm going to make it happen.

No one involved in her torture and self-loathing will survive by the time I'm through with them.

"Jesus," Dad curses under his breath, but I hear it and smirk.

He may not like knowing there's someone else who knows that he's my father, but he's also aware of just how much Melanie has come to mean to me in such a short time. Even if it doesn't make sense to him because he's never felt this type of connection before, he stands by me.

"Mel," I hedge, trying to gauge how she'll take what I need to tell her.

She's a lot stronger than she believes herself to be right now. Anyone who takes the time to look deep into her eyes will see the strength she holds inside of herself. It's the type of strength that comes from adversity, like watching a beloved parent die before your eyes, withering away to nothing.

"Yeah?" she asks, the tears making her voice sound thick.

I look at Dad and he nods his head to me, acknowledging that he approves of Melanie knowing the truth about him and our family.

Because I know that, even if she doesn't want anything to do with me, she'd never tell anyone a secret that could endanger our lives. That's just not the type of person she is.

"What's going on, Dari?" she asked, and my heart beats a little faster at the nickname she just used without thought.

Does she know she's making it impossible for me to stay away? Her sweet soul is a beacon to my darkness. I want to envelop her in the safety of its wings and keep her there, hidden from anymore cruelties the world wants to throw at her.

But I need her to accept me first, and she won't be

able to do that until I give her the bare and honest truth of who I really am.

"I think I love that nickname," I tell her, standing and moving to sit beside her on the couch, never once letting go of her hands.

I want the contact to make her feel safe and cared for, and the longer she looks into my eyes, the less tension seems to be in her shoulders. I'm going to take that as a win.

She blushes, quickly shooting a look at Dad that makes me smile. "He's not going to hurt you," I tell her gently, and Dad's eyes widen.

"It's not my style to harm someone who means anything to Daria. As long as you don't hurt her, you're safe." His voice rumbles, and the look on her face shows she's clearly terrified of him.

It's not an uncommon reaction. I've seen a lot of the recordings for his board meetings, so I know this is normal, but with everything that's happened to her, she has even more reason to be afraid of men then normal.

I groan. "Dad, you can't say it like that when she's just gone through what she has!" I snap at him, and he blinks at me.

"I—it's fine," Mel cuts in. "I'd never hurt you anyway." Her voices ends on a squeak, and I want to throttle my father. Fuck's sake.

"I know you wouldn't, and Dad doesn't make a habit of hurting women unless they're really bad people. Like, so bad they have a special seat in Hell waiting just for them. And he never hurts children," I say, then remember I haven't even told her about us yet, and I'm here spouting out random shit about killing like it's just another fucking Tuesday.

"Jesus, Daria. What is wrong with you?" Dad grumbles, and I shrug.

"She ties me up in knots. She's like my own personal truth serum," I admit, and he watches me closely for a moment.

"I am?" Mel asks quietly, her tears drying up now that the conversation has moved away from what happened to her.

"You are. It's fucking odd, and I don't know how to react to it," I say. "I've never had a problem keeping our family secret or keeping people away from us, but you're different." I swallow the thickness in my throat and check in with Dad once more to make sure he's truly fine with me telling her.

This is a huge deal to tell someone either of us barely know, but Dad already had Carlos do an extensive search into Melanie and her parents. I'd say it's a horrible invasion of privacy, but I get it. His first priority has always been to keep me safe, and he had the report before I ever stepped foot on campus last week and met her.

"Dari," Mel whispers, squeezing my hands. "I'm scared." Her lip trembles, and fuck, it's going to be my undoing.

"Shit," I curse myself out, fighting a war inside my head.

I don't want to tell her because she'll think I'm a monster, and I'll lose the one person I have actually felt an emotional connection to. I also don't want her to see Dad as a horrible person because he's not.

"Daria, it needs to be done," Dad says gently, and I nod.

"Melanie, I'm not who you think I am." I watch, waiting for the sadness to come from my lying to her, but it's not there. There's only confusion staring back at me.

"I mean, I know you lied about your childhood." She cuts a look to Dad. "I sort of understand why." There's a deep frown on her face that says she really doesn't, but that's because she's missing the biggest piece of the puzzle.

"Mel, can you look at me?" I ask her, waiting until her eyes are on mine. "The reason you don't really understand why Dad has gone to such great lengths to make sure no one knows about me isn't because of his tech job," I tell her, taking a deep breath.

"O…kay?"

"It's in case someone finds out about his other identity and job, then makes the connection. It would put Mom and I in danger, and he has done everything he can to avoid that. To keep me safe," I tell her, waiting for the words to sink in.

"Other job? Other identity?" she says, shaking her head. "What are you talking about, Daria? Can you just spit it out? I'm too exhausted to connect the dots here."

I take a deep breath and squeeze her hands once more before pulling mine away and telling her the truth.

"Dad is a contract killer, Melanie. And I'm following in his footsteps."

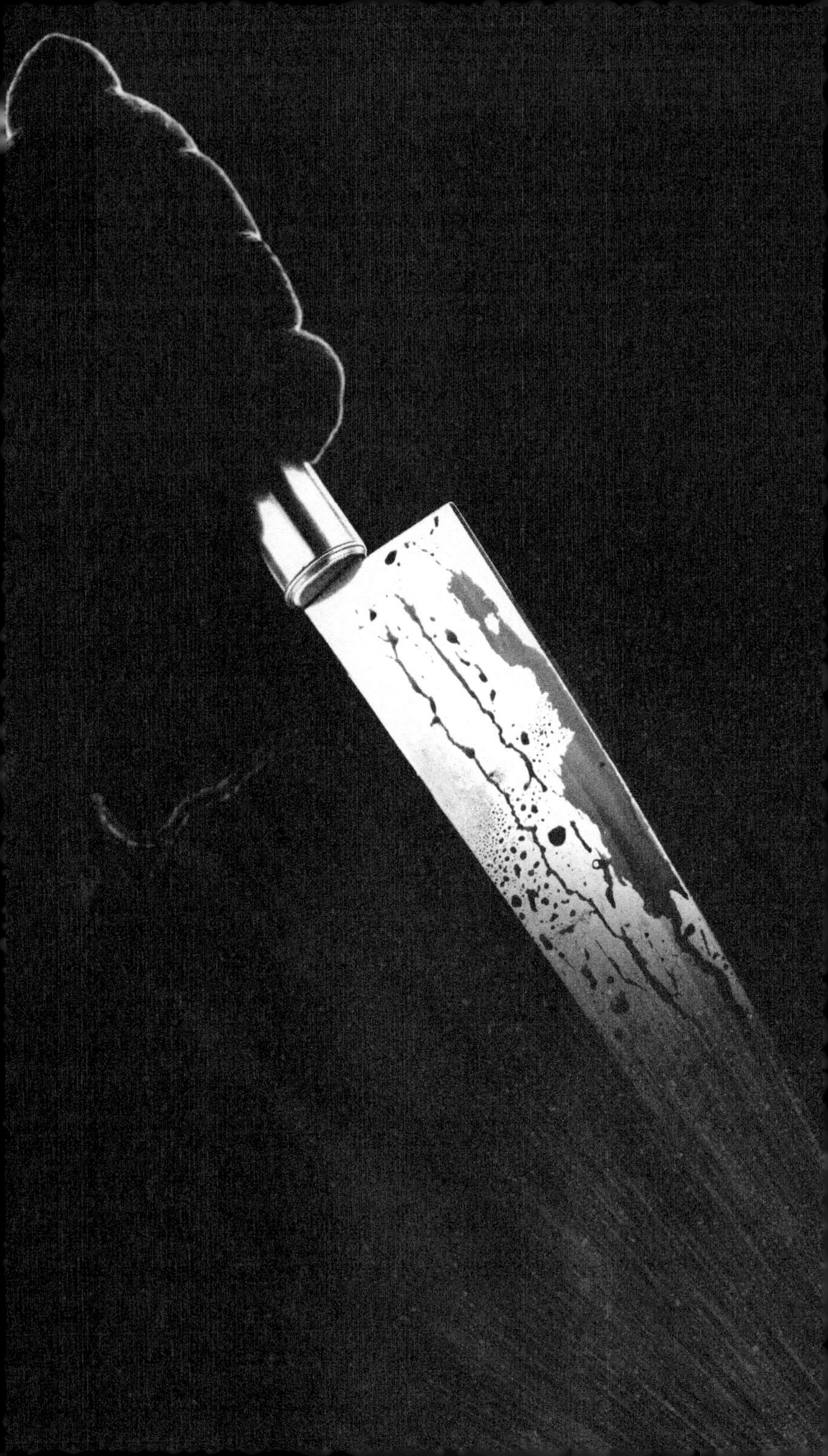

CHAPTER 16
MELANIE

What. The. Fuck have I gotten myself into?

Am I still sleeping, and this is some weird, twisted, fucked up dream? Is this another way for my brain to attack me after everything that has happened?

The seriousness of Daria's face says it's not, and one look at Kane is all I need to know that she is very serious about this.

She's a killer. Or protege maybe? Apprentice? Jesus Christ, I don't even know what to think right now. I'm sitting in a room with murderers. When did this become my life?

"I—I think I need to leave," I croak out, feeling myself shake in fear.

"Mel," Daria whispers as I stand up.

The pain in her voice gives me pause, and I look

down at where she's still sitting. She won't fight me if I want to leave, but I can tell by looking at her she doesn't want me to go.

"Dari," I say, shaking my head. "I—I don't understand," I whisper back, frozen in place as everything sinks in. "I just… this doesn't make any sense," I cry, letting my confusion and pain show.

"Melanie," Kane says, his voice dark, striking fear in me like nothing ever has. "Sit down."

I swallow, unable to hide my fear, but I still do as he says, sitting back down on the couch but pulling myself into the corner as a way to protect myself from him.

"Mel," Daria says my name again, trying to bring my focus back on her. Once I look at her, she continues. "Remember how Dad said I was attacked the same night everything happened?" she asks, and I jerk my head in acknowledgement.

My mind is swimming with panic, and her words barely register with me, but I try my best to focus on the girl I've shared a room with for the past week. A girl I was falling for. A girl I *am* falling for.

Oh my God, I'm falling in love with a killer.

"That was the first night I'd ever used the training Dad has instilled in me," she says, and my brain breaks a little.

Kane, the tech mogul of the world, has been

training his secret daughter how to become a killer. This isn't real. It can't be.

"What?"

She sighs, sharing another look with her dad, who nods at her before she turns back to me with a coldness in her eyes to match her father's.

"Matt sent three idiots to grab me in an alleyway. I heard them following me before I hung up with you, that's why it was so abrupt," she explains. I try to remember back to our phone call that night, but everything is muddled and twisted with rape, and it takes me a moment to sift through the memories.

I try not to get sick and breakdown over the images of Matt and Deedra holding me down while others watched and force myself to think back to the earlier phone call.

"You said you had to go and then hung up," I reply when I land on the right memory.

"Yeah. I'm a paranoid person, always paying attention to my surroundings because it's how Dad trained me to be in order to keep myself safe," she says, and I nod.

I eye Kane out of my peripheral vision. He's watching us with an intense stare like he may have to step in at any moment in order to protect Daria from me. As if I could ever harm someone trained to kill.

I couldn't even protect myself, so him seeing me

as a threat is a little overboard, but I can tell he loves her very much, so I let it go. I get the feeling he's probably like this with everyone. Or would be if anyone knew who she was.

"What happened?" I ask, relaxing my body just a little as I wait for her to tell me what happened to her.

The longer I sit here and push through the panic, I realize I'm not really in danger here. If they wanted to kill me, they've had two days to do it already. Why would they wait and let me crash here?

"Are you sure you want to know?" Daria asks me gently, and I nod.

"I have to know. I—I need to know where all of this is coming from to try and understand," I whisper, and she smiles but it doesn't reach her eyes, and my chest tightens a little. I don't like that sadness in her eyes.

"I've made the walk to Dad's place from so many different areas in the city, I knew exactly where they'd try to attack." She sighs, looking tired like she hasn't been sleeping. It's then I realize that this whole thing has been hard on her as well, just in a different way.

I feel like a selfish asshole for not asking her more about the attack, but I don't think I could have handled what she's about to tell me. I'm not sure I can handle it now, but we both know it's come to the point where I have to know.

I need all of the information in order to make a decision that could ultimately change my life forever. "I'll be okay, Dari. I need to hear it," I tell her.

Kane makes a sound of anger, but I don't move my eyes off of hers, afraid I will chicken out and run before I get the truth.

"When I got into the alley, I started to walk faster. I was hoping they'd just go away if I didn't respond. I didn't want a confrontation. I wasn't even aware of who was following me because I didn't look back." She takes a deep breath, and Kane sits silent. I think maybe he's waiting to hear the details of everything as well.

"One of them tried to flirt with me. I ignored him at first, but he was persistent. When I turned him down, I felt someone grab my hair." She winces as though she's remembering the pain, and I understand that. It hurts like a bitch when your hair is yanked on.

"Prick," Kane snarls, making me jump.

Daria rolls her eyes but continues her story, never taking her focus off of me. "It was only him at first, but I knew from the footsteps there were more with him, so I had to wait them out. I had to get a good feel of the situation before I could know the appropriate way to respond."

"That's insane," I say, almost to myself.

What eighteen-year-old knows to do that? How to assess a scene around them before they react?

It's a good thing, but it's surreal to think about, and something I wish I'd done that night.

"I played along until they tried to drug me," she says, cutting through my thoughts.

"They did drug you," Kane growls, and I find myself angry along with him.

"They drugged you?!" I screech, sitting up straighter.

She nods. "Yeah. Not a lot because I moved, but yes. It's… it's why I was too late." Her voice breaks, and she looks away from me.

"Too late?" I question, feeling lost again.

"Daria took the men out and was able to call me, but she passed out afterward. When I got there, the men were dead, and she was unconscious," Kane tells me in a matter-of-fact voice.

Holy. Shit.

Crap. I'm cursing a lot, but dang it! If there's ever a time to curse, it's now. "You… you killed three men while you were drugged?" I ask, the shock clear.

I don't know what shocks me more. The fact that she took three men on by herself and killed them all, or that she did it while drugged. Like, holy crap!

"Yeah," Daria admits, watching me closely.

"Are you a ninja or something?" I blurt out before I can stop myself, and she snorts.

"I think she's in shock," Kane says, clearly to Daria, and I think he's right.

"I'm not a ninja. I've just had years of self-defence training." She moves closer to me slowly, worried I will flinch away, but I'm too stunned. I'm too invested to move, whether it's shock or something else, I'm not sure.

"Right," I manage to say.

"I was too late to save you from him. By the time I woke up in Dad's car and worked out their threats about Matt through my muddled brain, I knew you were in danger. But I was too late," she says, looking angry.

So angry.

"It's not your fault," I tell her, feeling the need to assure her.

Her eyes narrow as her jaw sets. "Nor is it yours," she seethes, making me swallow. "But I will make them pay, Mel. Whether you walk away from me or not, I need you to know that I am going to take care of them," she promises.

"We will," Kane says, and I look at him.

"You're going to kill them? H—how?" I ask.

He smiles darkly, and Daria cackles beside me, the sound vibrating through me.

"We don't have a plan yet, Mel. But I promise you, they will know more pain than you did."

I look at Daria in shock, feeling lightheaded. "What do you mean?"

"The less you know the better," Kane tells me, and Daria nods.

I look between them, my head beginning to pound. "I think I need to lay down. I need… I need time to think about everything," I respond, looking Kane in the eye directly and ignoring the fear he instills in me with just a look. "Can I stay here while I figure this out?"

"If you want to, of course. You're safe here, Melanie. As long as you're in my house, no harm will come to you."

I believe him.

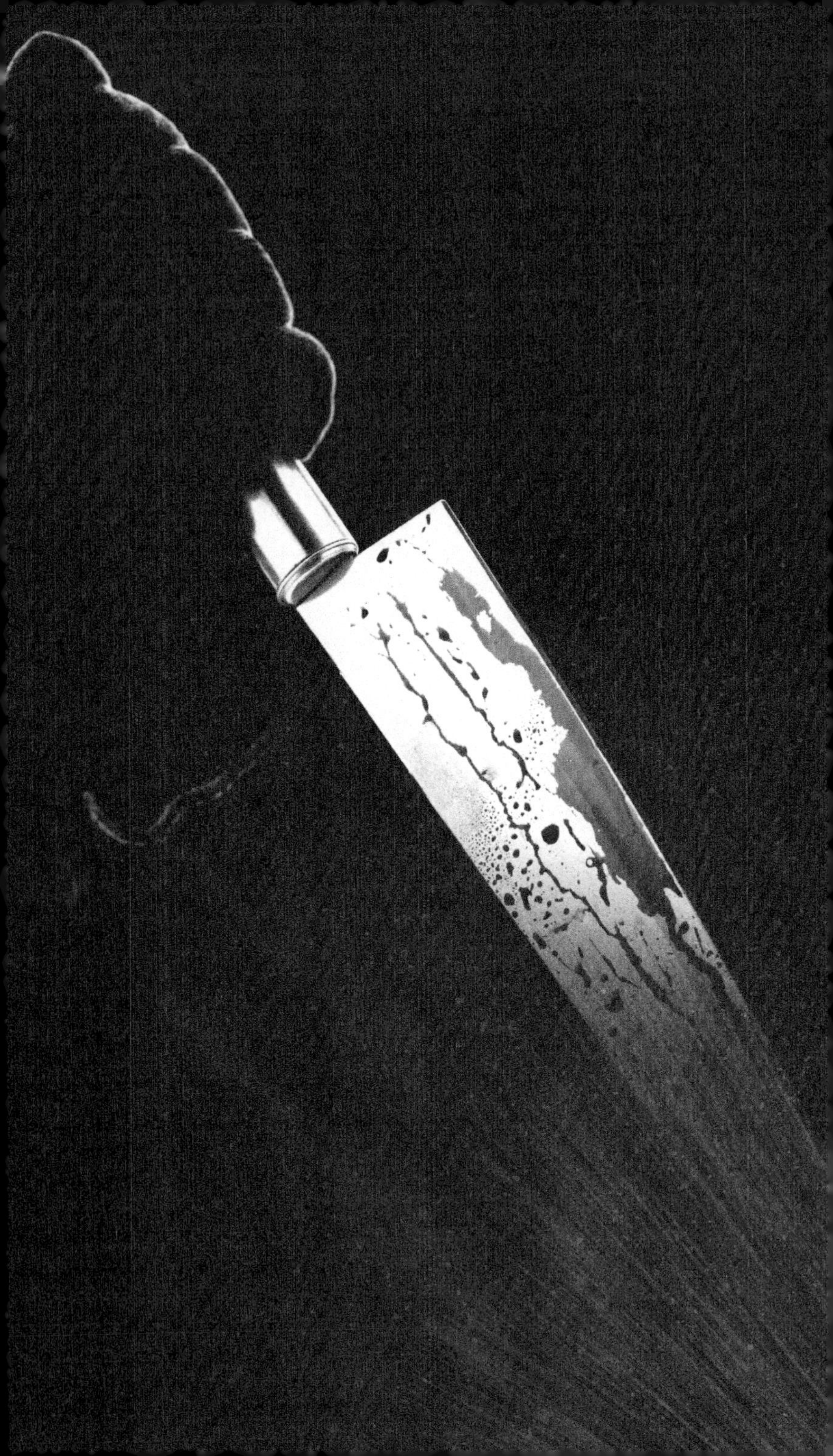

CHAPTER 17
DARIA

Once Melanie has gone back to the bedroom, I take a deep breath and move over to sit beside Dad.

"That went... I don't know how that went," I say, sighing.

I'm fucking exhausted and haven't slept since the night of the attack. I've been too worried about her and planning out exactly how I'm going to kill each and every one of those sick fucks.

"She's still here, sweetheart. That's a good sign," Dad says, dropping his hand on my knee to give it a squeeze.

"She's in shock, Dad. Like actual, full-blown shock."

He sighs, tired as well. He's been working every night to make sure the mess of bodies I left in that alley are truly dealt with. He doesn't want to leave anything to chance. I love him for that, but he needs to get some sleep too.

"She's been through a lot over the last couple of days. So have you." He shoots me a stern look. "How are *you* holding up with it all?"

I know he's asking me how I'm feeling about killing those three. I want to just ignore the question and live in denial, but I won't. Dad can see through my bullshit, anyway, so no point in trying.

"I think I'm okay. I regretted killing them for a while because I could have handled it better, but after everything that I've pieced together from Mel? I have no remorse because they'd have wound up on my kill list anyway." I look at him and smile. "I'm just sorry you had to clean up my mess."

He chuckles, pulling me into a side hug. "I would have killed them for daring to touch you, even if you hadn't."

That warms my heart. "I had a feeling," I tease with a smirk when I pull back.

His face becomes serious as he turns his body into mine, and I know exactly where this is going next.

"Have you given anymore thought to how you'd like to handle the bystanders?" he questions me, knowing I already have dark plans for Matthew and Deedra.

I've been thinking about the revenge I would serve on Melanie's behalf, but it's harder to gauge what is justified for watching. I can't torture them the way I will the ring leaders, but I don't want them to die easily either.

It's a hard call.

"I have an idea, but I'm not sure how doable it is without leaving a paper trail."

"Let me worry about that," he says, smiling at me. "I've been thinking about this whole college thing."

"Oh?" He has my full attention, and he knows it.

"What if you switched to online courses and started working for me sooner," he hedges, and I frown.

"I was hoping you'd say I could quit school," I groan, making him laugh.

"We both promised your mother that you'd graduate, but after the other night, I think she'd be open to you moving to online studies while working at the office."

"The real office? Or the office office?" I question, really hoping he says the latter.

"Both. I think hands on learning at the office will teach you more about taking over the company than any class will. I've spoken to a few of the board members about having a couple of interns brought in to shadow me, and they've agreed it could be beneficial to the company," he says smugly.

"Two?"

"You and Melanie. If she wants the job, that is."

"I don't know what her plans are, but I doubt she'll go back any time soon. I have to get her to call her Dad," I say, my chest feeling heavy.

I don't think she wants him to know what happened to her, but I also know how close they are, and he would want to know if she's hurting or had been hurt.

"Give her time to work through it. That's a family matter," he reminds me, and I nod.

"I know. Trust me, I know better than to get involved with this. It's up to her."

Dad looks at his watch, wincing. "I have to go. Are you alright here?" he asks, his eyes darting toward the bedrooms before landing back on me.

"I'm good. I think I may actually try and rest."

"You need to, or you'll be no good to help her." He kisses my head before grabbing his briefcase and heading to the door. "Call me if you need me."

"I will. Love you, Dad."

"Love you too, kid."

"NOOOOO STOP!"

A shrill scream jolts me awake. I'm not sure how long I was asleep for, but it's still daylight out which means Dad isn't home yet.

"PLEASE!" Melanie screams again, and I jump out of bed and run to her room, pushing the door open.

"Mel!" I scream as I climb onto the bed with her. "Baby, you have to wake up," I gently touch her shoulder. When she flinches away from my touch, I have to remind myself it has nothing to do with me. She's dreaming about them.

"Please don't. God, it hurts, please stop!" she cries and begs.

I hate to think she's fighting back in her dreams because she didn't fight back when it happened. Her earlier confession gutted me to my core, knowing she couldn't bring herself to fight then.

"Baby, it's me. It's Daria. I need you to wake up," I say a little louder, giving her a small shake.

Her body tenses for a split second before she bursts into tears, clearly awake.

"Make this stop. Daria, please make the pain stop," she whispers, curling into herself.

I lay on my side, gently nudging her to roll over and face me before I curl around her shaking frame.

"They'll never hurt you again, baby. I promise you that."

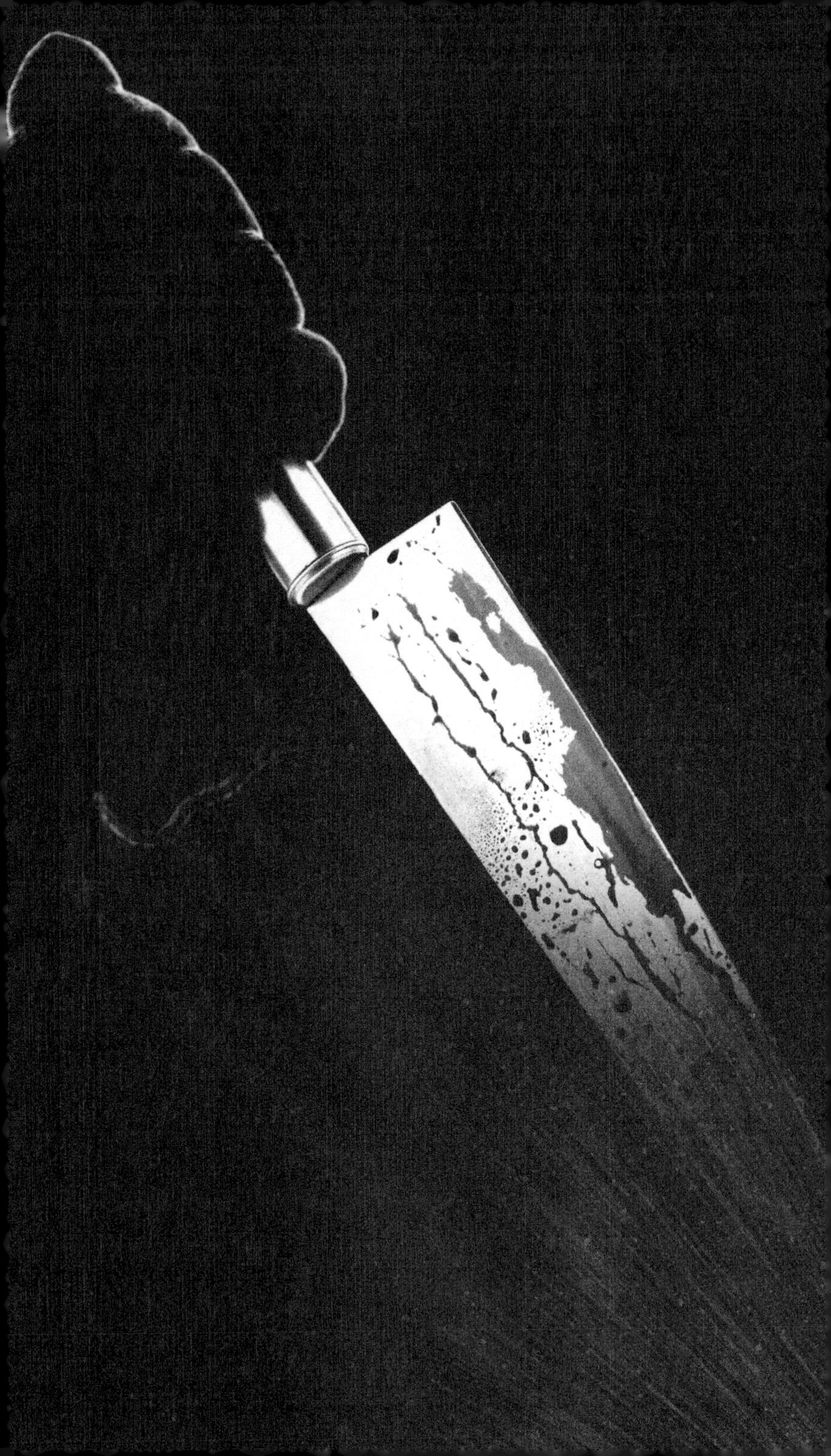

CHAPTER 18
MELANIE

I want the nightmares to stop.

I want to wake up and feel like me again without living through the horrors on repeat, like it's some form of torture session. It's not fair.

They'll never hurt you again, baby. I promise you that.

Daria's words play on repeat in my mind as the tears stop falling. Her heartbeat against my ear is more calming than anything else I've tried over the past couple of days, and I've tried everything.

I've gone through every sound on my meditation apps, from white noise to gentle flute music and everything in between, and nothing has helped. Nothing has calmed me.

Except Daria.

I don't know how long I was asleep this time

before the nightmares took over, but I gave everything a lot of thought before I fell asleep. At least, once the shock of their news wore off a little.

"Thank you for coming to help me," I whisper against her chest, and she tightens her hold on me.

"I'll always come for you if you need me, Mel," she whispers back. "As long as you want me to." She pulls away enough to look down into my eyes.

"I don't feel safe anywhere else right now," I whisper. "But, Daria, this is insane. How do I even begin to understand any of this?" I ask her, my mind filled with so many questions and thoughts.

She bites her bottom lip, trying to figure out how to describe this entire situation, but there is no perfect way that will have me magically understanding.

"Rip the band aid off," I tell her, and she blows out a breath and nods.

"Right, okay. To put it as simply and innocently as I can, Dad is a contract killer. The best," she says, her pride clear as she talks about him.

"And your mother knows this?" I ask, baffled.

She snorts, laughing as she shakes her head. "No. I mean, yes, she knows now. But when they met, she only knew him as the tech guy. They weren't planning me," she explains.

"Right. She's alright with this?"

She shrugs. "That's just always how it's been.

Dad wanted to be in my life, but there was a high cost to that. Hence no one knowing he has a child. Mom agreed that as long as he kept me safe and out of harm's way."

"Not to point out the obvious or anything, but you doing what he does doesn't exactly feel like you're staying out of harm's way," I tell her before I can think better of it, but she just smiles at me.

"Dad and I have always had one rule. No secrets. That means he had to be honest with me about who he is. I grew up knowing the truth so I could be aware of the dangers I could possibly face one day," she explains, and I find myself nodding.

It makes sense, what she's telling me. Doesn't make it any less fucked up or weird to me. It's hard to wrap my head around any of this.

"Would you have told me if the other night hadn't happened?" I ask quietly. I don't even know which answer I want from her, I just know I want the truth.

"Someday," she whispers back, moving in close to me again and cupping my cheek. "I didn't want to tell you because you're innocent, Mel. We tend to stay away from innocents."

"You really killed three of his friends by yourself?"

"Yeah, I really did. And it was my first kill, in case

you were wondering." She's trying to be open and honest with me, and I'm glad because now it allows me to be the same.

"I can't be in that world, Dari," I explain, touching my forehead to hers.

"I understand." Her voice breaks as she tries to pull away.

I shake my head and hold onto her tighter, trying to get my brain and mouth to work together to have her understand what I'm trying to say.

"No. I—I didn't mean I don't want you to be in my life, I just mean… whatever this is," I wave my hand between us, "I don't want to know the details of that part of your life." Shoot, I'm saying this all wrong.

"I'm a little confused," she admits, and I groan.

"I mean, I want to see where we go, if you want to. But I don't want the details of what it is you do." I try to word it without sounding like a complete tool, but I'm fairly certain I fail.

She smiles, moving until our chests are pressed together and our legs tangled. Her lips are only a few centimetres away, and having her so close is short-circuiting my brain a little.

"Just the stabby parts?" Her lips quirk at her own words.

"Uh, yeah. Those parts are something I just don't see myself ever being able to handle."

Her nose nudges against mine, causing my breath to hitch in my throat as my entire body comes alive.

"Can I kiss you, Mel?" she asks, moving her eyes to meet mine.

"Please." I barely get the word out before her lips gently cover my mouth like she couldn't wait to kiss me.

Her lips move over mine a few times, soft and eager while her hand still holds my cheek. It takes me as second before I remember I should be kissing her back.

Pressing myself into her more, I take her shirt in my hand and kiss her harder, deepening the push and pull of our lips before she's running her tongue along the seam, seeking entrance to my mouth.

I open up for her and move my hand to her neck as our tongues slide against one another. Daria growls, kissing me harder as her hands move into my hair and tug.

"Shit," I groan, and she chuckles, the air hot brushing over my lips before she kisses me again.

"That's so goddamn cute," she says before moving back in until we're both breathing hard.

"What is?" I ask, pulling back to look at her face. Her lips are swollen and glossy and so damn hot. I want to kiss her again and feel her hands all over my body.

At that thought, my heart seizes in my chest, and I stop breathing.

Memories flood me of Deedra holding me down as her boyfriend moved his hands all over my body, roughly ripping off my clothes. The panic I feel making it impossible for Daria to answer me.

"Baby," I think I hear Daria say. "Come back to me, Mel. I need you to breathe and come back to me."

I shut my eyes to try and shove the memories away. I don't want them to ruin this moment, or for Daria to think I'm more trouble than I'm worth.

"Dammit!" she curses, moving until I feel her hands cupping my face. "You are not more trouble than you're worth, Melanie Mahone, now open your goddamn eyes and look at me. See who's touching you right now," she orders, and surprisingly, the harsh tone has my eyes flying open until they land on hers.

I swallow, unable to speak. The worry and anger she feels is so clear on her face that I should be afraid, yet it calms me. Her words sink into my muddled thoughts, chasing away the darkness that was trying to once again consume me.

"Good girl," she praises, and even in my state of

panic, those words do something to me. They make me feel like I'm cherished and not a huge screw up.

She shakes her head at me before straddling my hips, the movement causing a short moment of panic before I lock eyes with her again, reminding myself who is with me.

"You wanted to know why Dad does what he does, and why I want so badly to follow in his footsteps?" she asks, and I frown, trying to clear my head.

Oh. We're back to the conversation before the kiss. Right.

"Yes," I croak, my voice betraying me, showing I'm not as steady as I want to be right now.

"Because sometimes it's the innocent who need the darkness to protect them." She leans down to kiss me gently before pulling away just a smidge. "You're an innocent, and you got hurt. Dad? He rids the world of bastards that don't have a right to be breathing the same air as you. I want to do that, too." She takes a deep breath and tears brim my eyes. "Let me be *your* darkness, Mel. Let me chase your nightmares away. Let me protect you."

Oh, God, my heart.

I sniffle, nodding my head because I think I love this woman who refuses to see me as the broken mess I am right now. She still sees the woman I was when she met me, and that means everything.

"Okay."

She smiles, leaning down to kiss me again. "Okay."

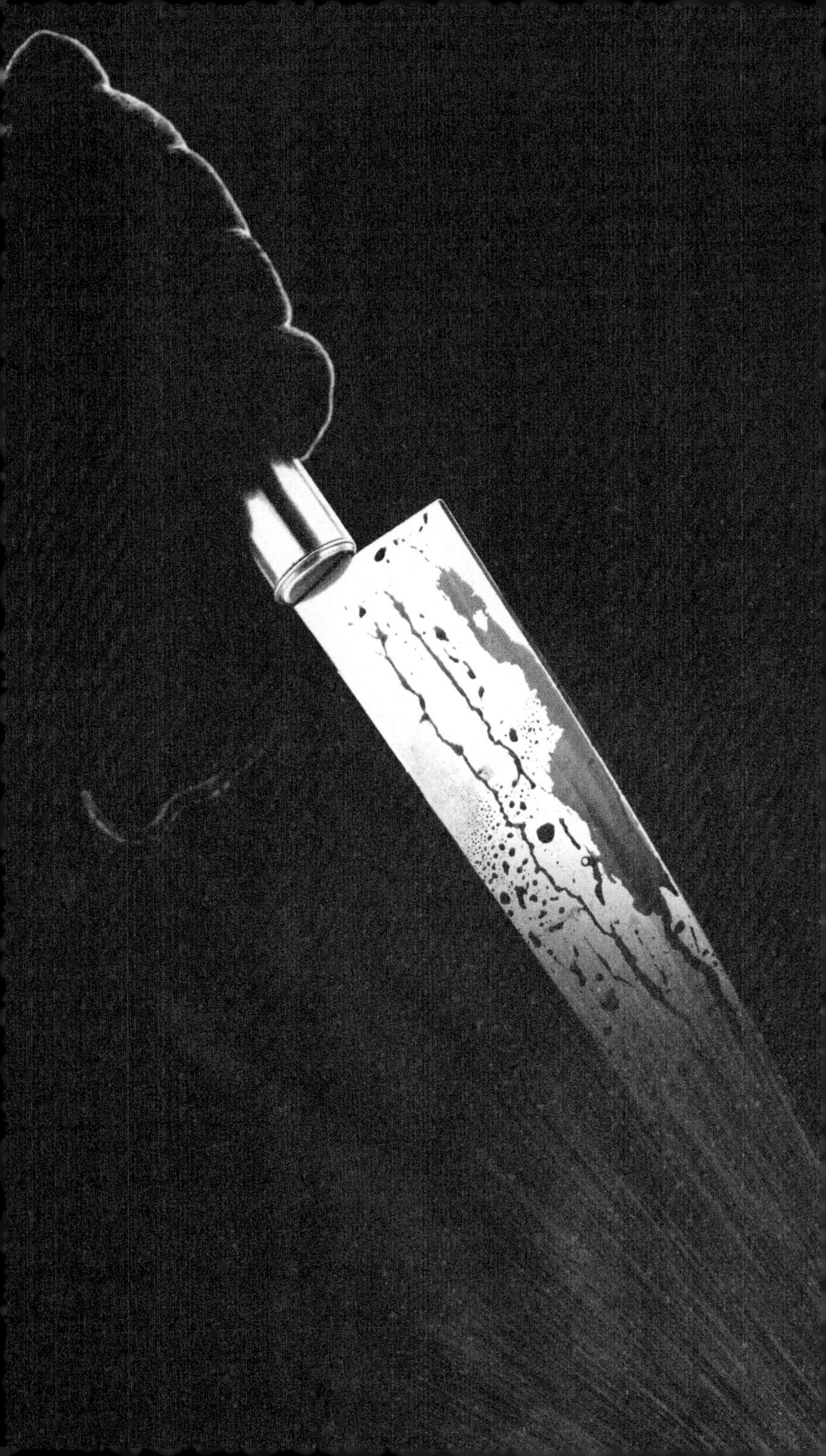

CHAPTER 19
DARIA

"That's it, Mel. You've got it! Harder. Punch that bastard in the face until you lodge a piece of his nose into his skull!" I yell at my girlfriend, encouraging her as she spars with Dad.

Once she agreed to be mine and let me fight the darkness for her, she seemed to relax a little. We fell asleep together, cuddled up in each other's arms and ended up sleeping for hours. No nightmares for my baby, and no insomnia for me.

It's taken a couple of weeks for her to feel safe enough around Dad to start training in the gym, but self-defence is something I know she wants to learn. And Dad has a black belt in kickboxing and Karate, so we don't even have to be around others.

"Jesus, Daria," Dad grumbles, ducking from Melanie's swing as I start to laugh. "I'm not the test dummy. She can save the actual violence for them," he says, making Melanie giggle.

God, it's a good sound to hear after everything.

"I don't know, Mr. Fitz," she teases him, circling the mat. "You're a pretty big dude. I doubt I'd even leave a dent," she says, and Dad stops to narrow his eyes at her.

"Now you listen here, ki—"

I watch with pride and laughter as she drops to the ground and sweeps her feet out to knock Dad on his ass.

It's not a very clean move yet, but the shock on Dad's face actually has me falling to the floor, laughing and gripping my stomach.

"Psych," Melanie says sweetly, and I curl up, laughing even more.

"You should… see… the look… on your face!" I tell Dad through wheezing breaths.

Dad shakes his head, grumbling about pain in the ass kids as he gets back on his feet. "Okay, you got me. But I don't want to hear that shit from you again, alright?" he says to Mel sternly, and she sobers up a little and nods.

"Sorry."

"No, don't be sorry. You sidetracked me to get me off of my game, and it was a good call." He acknowledges how well she did, and the smile on her face is everything. "I just don't want you to believe any of the shit you just said. What we're teaching you here is how Daria got the jump on those guys in the alley."

I told Dad about Melanie not wanting to know about the darker parts of what we do, so he's been careful with how he words things when she's around, proving he's coming to care for my girl too.

"Right." Mel winces as her face clouds over with memories of that night.

Dad and I share a look before I move over to her and pull her into my arms from behind, her back to my chest. "That's Dad's way of telling you he's teaching you how to be a ninja badass like me," I whisper into her ear, and she snorts.

"You already told me you're not a ninja, Dari," she teases, but the tension leaves her body, the memories momentarily forgotten. "But I'll agree with badass."

Dad chuckles, looking at the clock on the wall.

"Okay, girls. I have to go out for a job, and I believe you ladies brought some work home with you?" He raises an eyebrow, taunting me to take the bait, so I just narrow my eyes at him.

"Actually, we have classwork. We both have tests tomorrow, so we left work at the office," I remind him, and he smiles with a nod.

"Good. Go order a pizza or something, and study for whatever the hell it is you're studying."

Melanie laughs as she grabs her towel and water bottle off of the bench before we head back up to the apartment.

Pizza sounds really fucking good right now.

DAD:
> Have you started step one yet?

I check to make sure Melanie is paying attention to her books before answering.

ME:
> Yep. The sleezy prick is dying to get together for a "hangout".

DAD:
> No.

ME:
> Yeah, no shit. But I can still string him along until he's so desperate that he takes the invitations for him and his friends.

DAD:
> I've secured what you need. Now you just have to choose a time and date.

I smile wickedly, knowing exactly when I want this to happen.

ME:
Halloween.

DAD:
Good call. We'll make it happen, sweetheart. See you in the morning. I love you.

That makes me smile, like always.

ME:
I love you, too. Night, Dad.

DAD:
Night, kid.

"Is that your dad?" Mel asks, and I nod, putting my phone away.

"Yeah, he's just checking in with the plans I'm making, and saying goodnight." I'm careful with how I word it, not wanting to tell her details but not wanting to keep shit from her either. It's going to be a learning curve for the two of us, but we'll figure it out.

"I know I said I didn't want any details, and I don't. Just… promise me you'll tell me when I can stop being afraid of running into them on the corner?" Her voice is quiet, and I reach over to hold her hand.

"I promise." I close my psychology books, sick of studying. "As a heads up, you should maybe think about inviting your father here for Halloween?"

She drops her pen and stares at me with wide, unblinking eyes before swallowing deeply.

"Halloween. Got it," she squeaks, and I curse myself for mentioning it when there's still a few weeks left.

"Hey," I say, getting her attention as I shuffle over to her. "Don't think about it. I just didn't want there to be secrets between us. But if you'd rather not know any of it at all, we can discuss what that'll look like, too."

She clears her throat and leans into my touch. "No, you're right. I don't want there to be secrets between us either. If you're going out for something like that, maybe just refer to it as a job like your dad did tonight?"

"Okay, baby, I can do that."

She smiles gently, leaning in to kiss me, and I smile against her lips.

"Is he gone all night?" she asks, pulling back.

"Uh, probably. Why?"

We haven't done anything more than make out yet because I don't want to push her past her limits or possibly trigger her, so I'm not expecting the next words to fall from her gorgeous lips.

"I want to be with you, Dari," she sighs. "I don't know how far I can go, but I think as long as I keep my eyes on you, I'll be okay."

Just the thought of her under me, writhing with pleasure, is enough to make my clit throb.

"If you want to be cumming on my tongue and fingers, all you have to do is say so, Mel."

She blushes instantly, and I watch with rapt attention as her nipples harden against the thin camisole she's wearing.

"I believe I just did, babe."

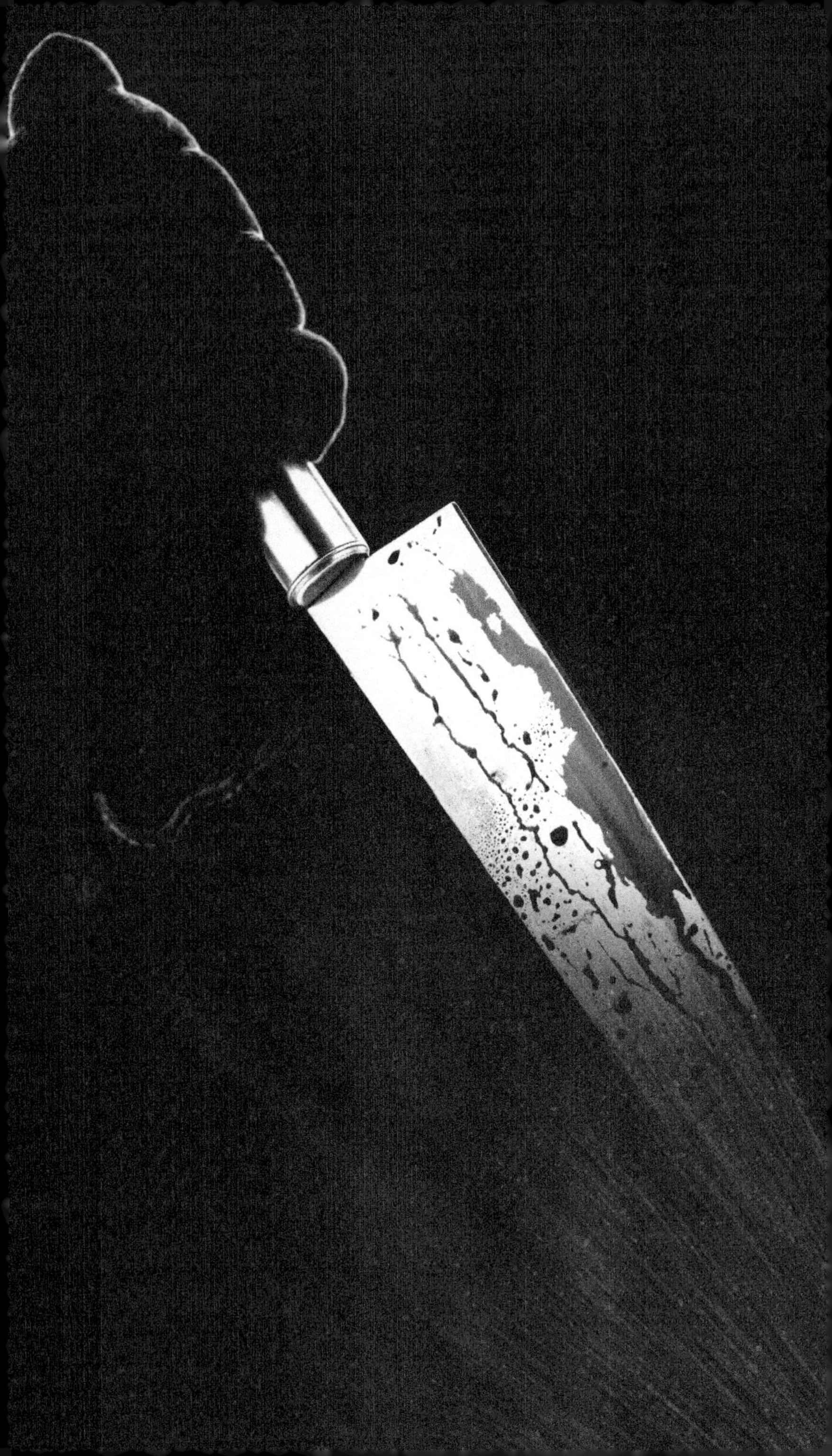

CHAPTER 20
MELANIE

As soon as we're in the bedroom, Daria pushes me against the door. She's kissing my neck while her hands trail down my waist, squeezing and pulling me closer.

I feel like we've been waiting for this moment for a lifetime rather than a few weeks. Sleeping together while being cuddled up every night has been the best kind of torture, and I wouldn't change it for anything.

Being in her arms makes the nightmares a lot less harsh. Add in the self-defence training I've been working on with her and Kane, and I've started to come back into myself a little more with each passing day. With every move I nail, I feel more like I'm able to protect myself from something like that happening ever again.

It's a powerful feeling.

"Oh, God," I moan when Daria nibbles my earlobe, moving her hands to squeeze my ass.

"Not God, but if you really want to call me something, you can call me Daddy," Daria says against my neck before chuckling.

"That a kink of yours?" I ask, not completely opposed to the idea if it gets my girlfriend off.

She just laughs, moving up to brush her lips against mine. "Nope, but it sounded hot in my head." She kisses me hard and pulls back again. "I'd rather you scream my name when I make you cum."

Oh, hell. "God, you're driving me crazy," I whimper, making her grin.

"Am I? I haven't even started yet," she teases.

Wrapping my hands around her waist, I move fast and spin us so she's the one leaning against the door, momentarily giving me control.

"Is that so?" I taunt with a grin.

"Ooo, my baby has some dominance in her?" Dari moans as I nip her lip.

"I need to taste you," I tell her, moving in to kiss her hard.

The second she opens up to me, my tongue caresses hers, memorizing the little sounds she makes as my hands wander all over her body.

I've held back until now, not wanting to get her

hopes up for more than making out, but I'm done with that. I fucking need her.

Daria groans when I cup her breasts and squeeze. "More," she pleads.

"Bed," I tell her, pulling us away from the door.

We move as one, stripping each other while trying not to break our heated kiss. By the time we've made it across the room, we're bare from the waist up, and I take a moment to really look at her.

"You're so damn beautiful," I gush, my eyes almost tearing up.

She is, though. She's not just sinfully hot, but there's a radiant confidence about her that is truly breathtaking to me.

"You're the beautiful one, baby," she says, moving to push me onto the bed before leaning down to kiss me softly. "And I'm the luckiest bitch alive that I get to have you."

I huff out a dry laugh, shaking my head, but she doesn't like that.

Dari reaches her hand into my hair and wraps it around her fist to pull on it, making me moan as she hovers over my face.

"Say it with me, Mel. I am gorgeous." She waits, but I don't realize she's serious until she pulls on my hair harder, bordering on painful. "Say it."

In this moment, I know I'd follow her to the ends

of the earth and back. She loves me enough to try to make me see what she sees when she looks at me.

"I am gorgeous," I whisper, my voice breaking.

She narrows her eyes at me. "Louder, baby. I want you to scream it until you fucking believe it."

I search her eyes, seeing her determination, and nod.

"I am gorgeous!" I say louder, and she kisses me hard, pushing her tongue past my lips while her other hand moves to the top of my sleep shorts.

"Mmm, that's a little better." Her hand moves past the waistband of my shorts and panties until her fingers gently brush against my clit.

"Shit!" I cry out, desperate for her touch. I've never felt this way before, like my entire body is a live wire.

"So goddamn wet for me," Dari growls, moving her fingers to play with me. "Say it again, Mel. Say 'I'm fucking beautiful and perfect' for me," she demands, her fingers sliding through my lower lips while her hand grips my hair tighter.

"Oh, hell," I moan, my breath kicking up a notch with how good she's making me feel. "I am beautiful and perfect!" I end on a scream when her finger circles my clit again.

"Not quite, Mel. Say it with conviction. I want you to know how fucking beautiful you are," Dari pants against my ear. "I want you to believe what I know to be true, and that's the fact that you bring me to my fucking knees with your beauty and strength."

She moves her finger down to my entrance, teasing me with her thumb on my clit.

"Oh, God. Oh, oh, please!" I ask, moving my hips until the very tip of her finger slides into me.

"Say it, Melanie. Say it and believe it, and then I'll treat this sweet cunt like it's the best gift I've ever been given." She nibbles my lip, breathing heavy against me. "I bet you taste so fucking good, baby. Say it."

She slides her finger further into me, and I repeat her words on a long groan.

"I'm fucking perfect and beautiful! Now please, for the love of all things holy, make me cum before I lose my shit!" I scream, and she thrusts her finger into me all the way while taking my mouth with hers in a brutal kiss that takes my breath away.

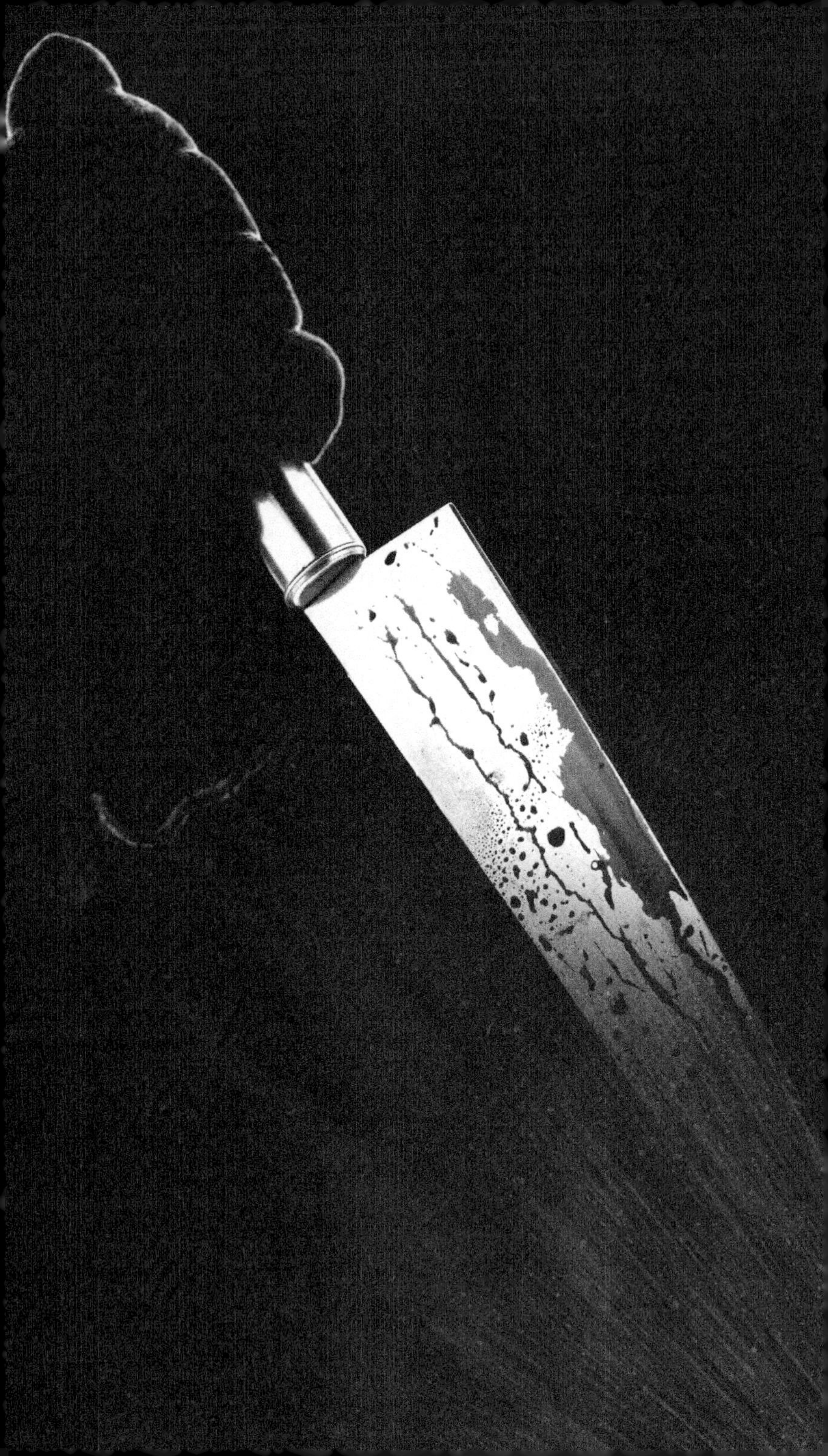

CHAPTER 21
DARIA

It'll take time to make Mel believe she's as gorgeous as I see her, but I will fight every goddamn day to make her see it because she deserves that self-love.

The second she screams how beautiful and perfect she is before begging me to make her cum, I'm beyond soaked and desperate for her.

"Fuck, yes, baby. That's it," I growl against her neck, pulling my finger out and adding a second, going slow to make sure I don't trigger her. "Eyes on me, Mel. If you take your eyes off of me, I stop." I want her here with me and nowhere else.

She feels so good squeezing my fingers as I pleasure her. I never want to stop if it means she looks at me like that for the rest of our lives together.

Jesus, she's sinful.

I bend down, keeping my eyes on hers while I

take a nipple into my mouth and suck at the same time my fingers plunge back into her. Her chest arches into me as she moans, struggling to keep her eyes on me.

"Good girl," I praise her. "You feel so good around me, Mel. I want you to cum for me," I rasp, biting down on her tit until she grunts, then I lick away the sting.

"Frig, that's, oh," she moans when I start pumping my fingers into her faster, determined to get her off before I take her shorts off.

I switch to her other nipple, giving it the same attention and living off of the sounds she's making. When her cunt squeezes my fingers, I bite into her flesh and she screams her release, gushing all over my fingers, and I damn near lose it.

I'm so needy for my woman that it's becoming a struggle to fucking think.

"Oh my God! Yes, holy shit, Dari! Fuck, hell, yes," she whimpers and moans as her body shakes from the power of her release.

I take in the beauty of the moment as her eyes close in euphoria. Her chest and face are a blushing pink that I want to lick and nibble on to mark her as mine.

It's too good of an idea to pass up, so I gently

remove my fingers from her entrance before pulling my hand from her pants.

"That was incredible," I tell her, and she chuckles breathlessly.

"Shouldn't that be my line?" she sasses, and my heart flutters.

I missed seeing her like this. Carefree and happy.

"It bears to be repeated anyway, so go for it." I taunt, moving my hand covered in her juices, wiping them across her collarbone before leaning in to lick them off of her while dragging my teeth across her delicate skin.

"So fucking delicious."

Her hands move into my hair, holding me to her for a moment before pulling me back up to her mouth and tasting herself.

Fucking hell.

I moan into her mouth and grind my hips into the bed, needing to feel some form of pressure on my clit. I don't think I've ever been as turned on as I am from watching Mel come alive under me. It's something I could easily become addicted to.

"My turn," she says with a smirk.

Her hand pushes against my shoulder, guiding me to lay on my back as she moves over me.

"Your turn?" I rasp. I'm not used to giving up control to anyone.

I'll let them fuck me with their fingers before getting each other off, but I've only let one other woman go down on me before. It takes a certain level of vulnerability to expose yourself to someone, and I've never been willing to do that with anyone else.

"Yeah, babe. My turn," she snarks as she works my yoga pants off of me, taking my underwear with them.

I feel exposed for some reason. Melanie is far from the first woman I've been naked in front of, but she is the first one I care about what she thinks.

"I'm going to Hell," she whispers the moment I'm free of all my clothing.

"Not likely," I joke, trying to ease my nerves.

She kneels on the floor in front of me, pressing my knees open until she's level with my soaked core.

"No, I'm most definitely going to Hell," she says, her eyes flicking up to look at me as she licks her lips. "I've decided your body is my new religion, because it is worth worshipping."

She blushes, but moves forward, kissing her way up my thighs as she moves my legs over her shoulders.

"Fuck," I hiss, dying to feel her mouth on me.

"Patience, Dari. I'll get there when I'm ready," she taunts, blowing air onto my lips.

My hips lift off the bed as I moan deep and loud, fucking needing her.

"Mel, baby, please," I plead as she teases me, nibbling my thighs. She's so close to my core, I can feel the heat coming from her.

"So polite," she teases, but moves her mouth to my centre.

The second her tongue touches me, I cry out in pleasure.

"Fuck," I curse when she pushes her tongue against me, pressing it harder against my clit. The sensation overwhelming me. "You're so good at that. Jesus," I curse again, and she groans, the vibrations coursing through my entire body.

"I want to taste every inch of you, Dari," she whispers, moving one of her hands off my hips to tease my entrance.

"Fuck. How did I go without this for so long? Oh!" I moan louder as she works her finger inside me until she's knuckle deep.

"What do you mean?" She pauses, pulling her mouth back to look up at me.

I shake my head, wanting to cry. I don't fucking cry. Ever.

"I've only given someone the opportunity to pleasure me this way once, Mel. I don't like being vulnerable for anyone, but you're different. I'm glad I have this with you."

Her eyes light up with fire before she devours me with her tongue, sucking and nibbling on my clit as her fingers curl inside of me, matching the tempo of her mouth until I'm a fucking mess.

"God, you're fucking heaven, babe," she moans, stiffening her tongue to flick against me in fast strokes until I'm screaming my release and soaking her face.

"FUCK!" I scream. "MEL, DON'T STOP. DON'T STOP!"

My hips grind against her face as my entire body locks up, spasming from the strongest orgasm I've ever had.

"Delicious," Mel groans, pulling back and standing to move up my body.

She kisses me hard, letting me taste myself on her tongue, and I'm done. I need to fuck her.

"Pants off, Melanie. Now."

I push her back onto the bed and make quick work of getting her shorts and underwear off. They're wrecked from her orgasm earlier anyway, and I take pride in knowing how well we burn together. We were made for one another.

I move to straddle her hips, winding our legs

together so I can grind against her when I drop down.

"Hey, Mel," I whisper, leaning down to kiss her.

"Yeah?" she whispers back, and I smile.

"I love you," I tell her the words my heart is begging me to scream from the rooftops so the whole world knows she's mine.

Her lip quivers as she looks into my eyes. "I love you, too."

She moves her hand to cup my cheek, and I kiss her softly, lowering my pussy to hers and groaning when we slide together.

"Yes, oh God," she rasps, lifting her hips to grind against me. It feels so perfect and incredible I let go and just feel.

"Perfect for me," I moan, pushing myself against her.

It doesn't take us long to find a rhythm. I ride her like she's the only thing that exists in this world while she sits up to start thrusting against me until the room is filled with sounds of our love and passion.

The slap of wet against wet as we build ourselves higher and higher, gasping for air between moans and kisses is heady, and the moment Mel falls over that edge, screaming my name, I lose all hold on reality.

"Mel! Fuck, yes, baby. God, you're perfect. So fucking good, cumming, covering me with your release." I pant and praise her as my pussy grinds against hers once more, forcing my body into another mind-blowing release. "Made for me. Perfect," I scream, riding that high.

"Oh, fuck. Shit, Dari. Yes, cum with me. I love you. I fucking love you," she cries out as we continue to rock against one another, slowly coming down from the high until I'm collapsing on the bed beside her, completely spent.

"I love you too, Mel," I say through heaving breaths. "So fucking much. It's terrifying," I admit, but she understands.

She rolls over, taking my face in her palms and running her nose against mine with a smile.

"Don't be afraid, Daria. Together, we're going to conquer everything."

I. DO. NOT. CRY. But in this the moment, I come really fucking close.

"Together," I whisper, feeling myself drifting off to sleep.

"Always."

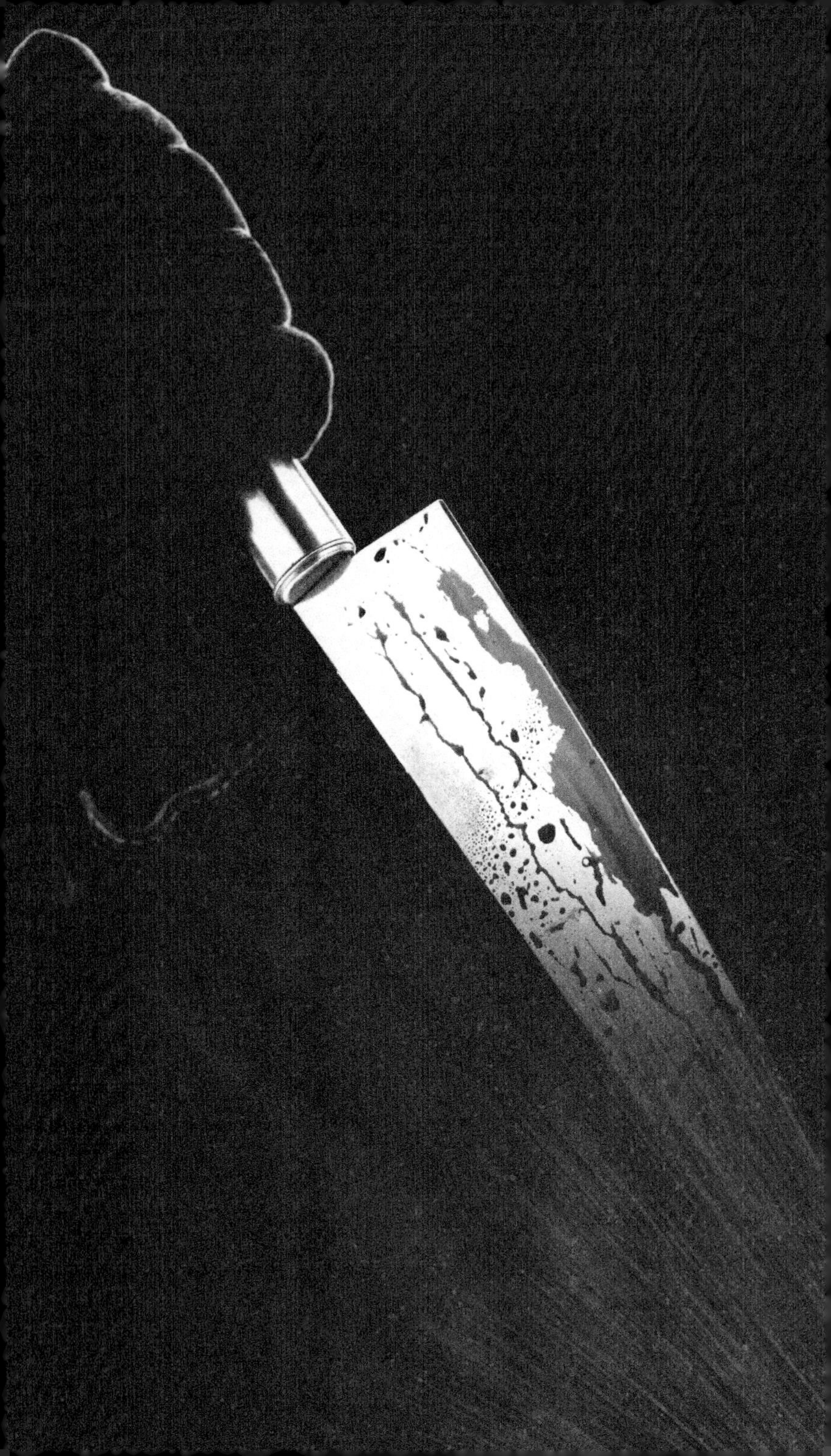

CHAPTER 22
DARIA

U̲g̲h̲.

SCUMBAG:
Hey sxy. How was your night?

I roll my eyes at Matt's pathetic attempt at flirting. I mean, really? Do women actually want to be spoken to that way? Geez. He can't even take the time to add one letter into sexy to make it a complete word. It's like he has zero brain power.

I gag, and Mel looks over at me with a raised eyebrow. "What's wrong?"

I groan, laying my head on the desk. We're at Dad's office, but he didn't come in today. He's on another business trip, this one for the company, but told us to stay put for this one.

Fine with me. It's a quick trip that would just end in insane jet lag, and I don't have the energy for that. When he has to leave for a few days, then he'll take us with him.

"Some guys are scum," I snark, and she chuckles.

"More disgusting messages, I assume?" she asks, but I just nod.

She's aware of what I'm doing to lure him into trusting me, or the fake me, at least. We don't keep secrets.

"I totally get why most women love older men, now. The younger ones are so fucking stupid."

She cackles at me, a huge smile on her face. "Not all guys our age are morons like him and his friends, you know. Look at Zach," she says, telling me about her best friend back home.

He's a good guy from what I can tell, and he at least speaks in full sentences. He's also extremely sweet to Mel, so I guess I can't group them all together.

"Point taken. I doubt Dad was ever this bad either. I just think my hatred for him is making this communication thing so much worse." I frown. "I know a couple of guys that are nothing like him, too. But the ones that are just irritate me."

She nods in understanding, the corner of her

mouth set in a smirk. I love that smirk because it means she's about to blast me with some of the sass I love so much.

"You're the one that already admitted to having a low tolerance for humans in general. I think you just don't like people," she says, and I tilt my head to the side.

"Correct. I really, really don't. But we both know this prick deserves everything I feel for him," I say, my voice dark and cold. It always is when I speak about them.

Before she can answer, someone knocks on the door to Dad's office before it opens. The vice president of the board walks in, smiling at us from ear to ear.

He has to be in his late sixties, but he's a sweet man. One of my favourite people here.

"Ladies," he nods his head in greeting, "how is everything in here?"

"It's going well. Mr. Fitzpatrick just had a conference call with us to check in about half an hour ago," I reply. Using Dad's formal name still feels weird, even after a few weeks, but it's getting easier.

Time is flying by, too. One more week until Halloween, and I can't fucking wait.

"Yes, he called me. I'm actually here because he

requested the two of you come and sit in on a business meeting I'm about to have. Think you could take some notes for an old man?" he teases, and we chuckle.

"Anything for you, Mr. Pine," Melanie says sweetly, and he beams at her.

"Thank you kindly." He looks at both of us before moving back to the door. "Conference room three in fifteen minutes. Thank you again, girls."

Once he's left us alone, I open my phone back up to text the scumbag.

ME:

> It was okay. Really busy and missing you ;)

SCUMBAG:

> We can fix that whenever you want, bby. Just say the word.

Idiot.

> **ME:**
> I'm actually invited to this super VIP Halloween party. I'm allowed to bring eight people. Think you have any friends you'd want to bring along?

> **SCUMBAG:**
> Fuck yeah! That's what I'm talking about. I gots a few in mind if you don't mind me bringing a few chicks from the sorority.

> **ME:**
> Perfect! Shoot me off the names, and I will add them to the list to get in! Can't wait to finally meet you! Remind me to send you the address tonight when I get home.

> **SCUMBAG:**
> Yeah, I'll shoot off the deets soon bby. Tlk l8r

"Gotcha, asshole," I whisper, my body flooding with giddiness that I'm so close to killing them all.

"You ready, Dari?" Mel asks, standing up from the other side of our shared desk.

She looks fucking sinful in that pencil skirt and blouse, and I'd love nothing more than to rip it off and taste her right now. But not in Dad's office.

As much as I'd love it, I know for a fact that man

has cameras in here, and that's the last thing he needs to see. Just the idea of Dad seeing me tongue fuck my girlfriend is enough to kill my libido.

"Ready." Maybe this meeting will fly by, and we can get home to more fun activities.

Yeah, that sounds like a plan to me.

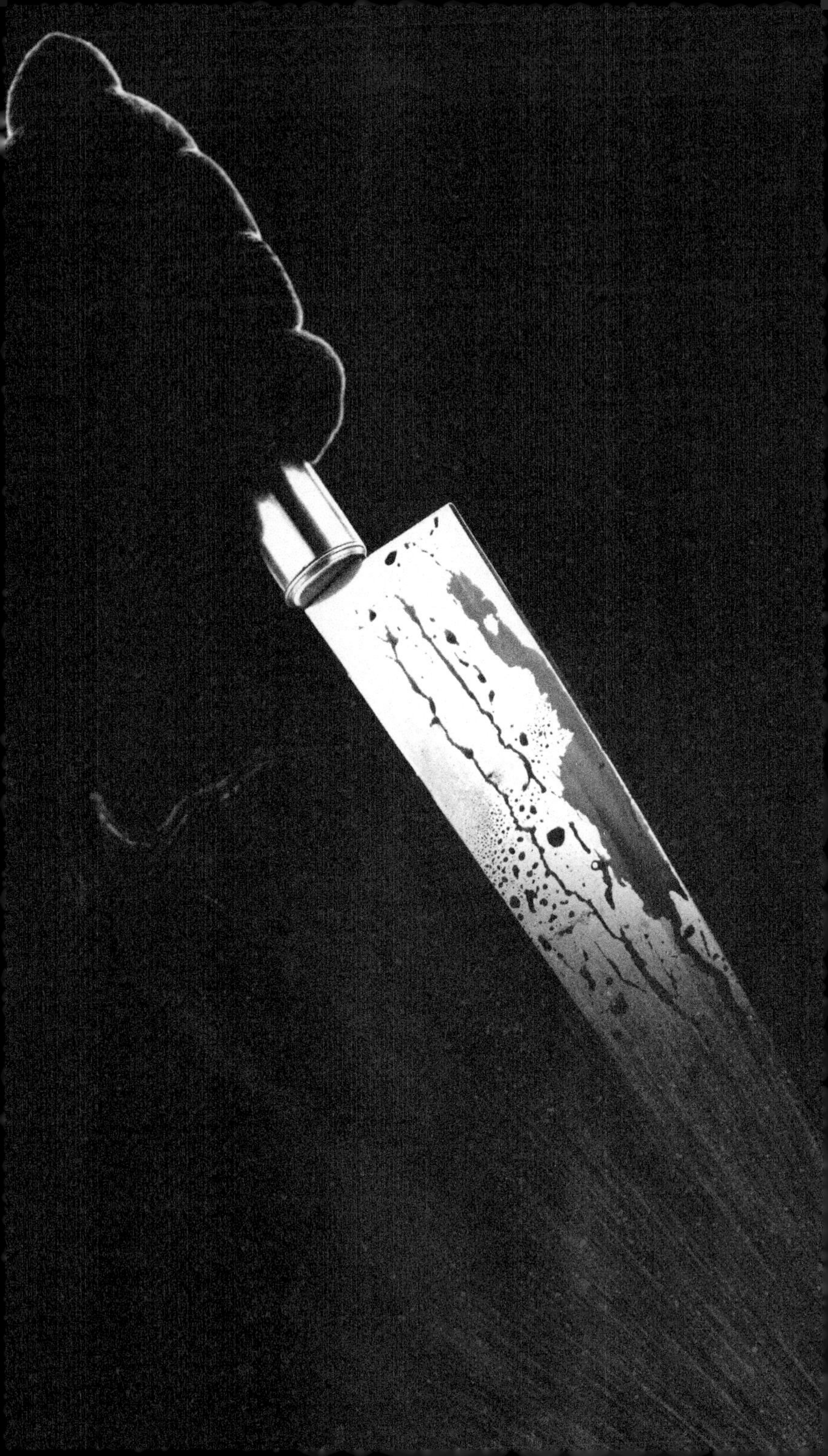

CHAPTER 23
MELANIE

I'm dying. I have to be.

"Harder, Melanie. Use your core!" Kane is barking out orders to me while we spar on the mats in his home gym.

The man owns the entire building and even has his own pool and gun-range in the basement.

He and Daria are the only ones with a key to make the elevator come down this far. The other tenants have to use the building's gym. I honestly don't see why he even lets anyone else live here if he's just going to be so paranoid over everything.

I made the mistake of saying that to Dari once, and she had an amazing laugh over it. She said his reasoning was sound enough. That an empty apartment building in the middle of the city would look too suspicious. As it is, he only rents the other condos out to businesses with employees that have to travel often. He makes sure they have a separate way to get in and out of the building than the entrance he and Daria use.

Apparently, it's a common practice for businesses like Kane Technologies to have these apartments in larger cities.

"I am using my core!" I growl at him, moving my leg to roundhouse kick him, but he grabs my foot and pushes it away with ease.

"You're not. Your movements are too choppy because you're not applying your core. If you take the strength from your core, you have the ability to move more fluidly and with more speed. Again." He claps his hands together, and I glare at him.

"Anyone ever tell you you're a slave driver, Mr. Fitz?" I growl, and Daria barks out a laugh where she's working with Carlos on the mat beside us.

"Watch Daria and try to mimic her movements," he says, moving to stand beside me as we focus on them.

"Show me what you've got, little Fitz," Carlos taunts Daria, but she just smirks.

"Now, now, Carlos. You know my last name isn't the same as Dad's," she replies, moving around him like she's on the hunt.

"And Prescott doesn't suit you. Now quit stalling and come at me."

Daria moves around him for a moment more before striking. I watch her as she whips around, lifting her leg up and hitting him in the back with enough force to knock him forward.

"That's my girl!" Kane whoops, chuckling as Carlos grumbles.

"Is he going easy on her?" I ask under my breath, and Kane shrugs.

"Honestly, it's impossible to tell. Carlos has been with me for many years and has a lot of the same training I've given Daria." He turns to look at me. "If they ever had to come to a head, I would say they'd be evenly matched. It would be a close call."

"But he's easily three times bigger than her," I point out, and he nods.

"True, but she's also learned to use her opponent's weight against them. Add on her fierceness, she'd be able to take him and come out the other side. Not that it will ever happen," he states, and I watch the woman I love with new eyes.

I pay more attention to her stance and movements, memorizing them to try and apply later.

"I'm ready," I tell Kane, taking a deep breath.

"Alright. One more go, then it's time for you girls

to study." He nods his head, then moves back to the centre of the mat.

Before I can get myself into the position I saw Daria in, she's behind me.

"You have to relax." Her hands move to my hips. "Take a deep, centreing breath," she guides, and I do. "Good, again."

I close my eyes, feeling the breath enter my lungs before I slowly let it out, the tension leaving my body to allow the muscles to relax more than they have all night.

"Like this?" I ask, keeping my eyes closed. I'm trying to not let this become sexual in front of Kane. If my mind goes there, I won't be able to hold the blush back.

"Just like that. Now, widen your stance until your feet are hip width apart," Kane directs, and I do as he says while Daria's hands hold my hips steady.

"Good," she says quietly for my ears only. "Now bend your knees. No, that's too much. Perfect," she praises me when I get them into the right position.

"Now, keep that stance in mind, then move your left foot in front of you so the stance is staggered rather than equal," Kane directs, and I nod.

I open my eyes, moving to stand how he says. When I get settled into that position, bouncing from one foot to the other, I can feel the difference. There's a power in this stance compared to how I was standing before.

"Wonderful, now try the kick again," Daria says. She moves her hand to my stomach. "Take a deep breath now."

"Okay." I do as she says. When my diaphragm extends, she presses in just enough that I can feel the pressure.

"Use these muscles. They're the ones that will give you more speed and stability," she says before moving back.

"I'll try, but I've never worked out in my life. I don't really have control over them the way you do," I admit.

"Then tomorrow we'll start doing yoga together. It helps build core strength and extend flexibility."

"That sounds like an excellent idea. Now, take that last roundhouse kick before we call it a night. Let's see the difference with the new stance."

I nod, getting myself ready before I twist around, lifting my leg and feeling the difference in how smooth I move when using my core.

"Better," Kane says, and I smile.

"I felt it. The difference. I thought I was using my core before, but I was trying to power through with my legs. That felt much steadier."

"Great job. See? We'll get you to badass ninja status in no time, baby," Daria says, and I laugh.

"Definitely." I keep laughing as Kane and Carlos shake their heads at us with smirks on their faces.

"Alright, you badass ninjas. Let's go grab some dinner before you two disappear on me."

"Food, yes!" Daria cheers, and I can't help the snort that leaves me. She shrugs at me in response. "Hey, I can't help it that I love food. It's my dirty mistress."

God, this woman is crazy, and I absolutely freaking love her.

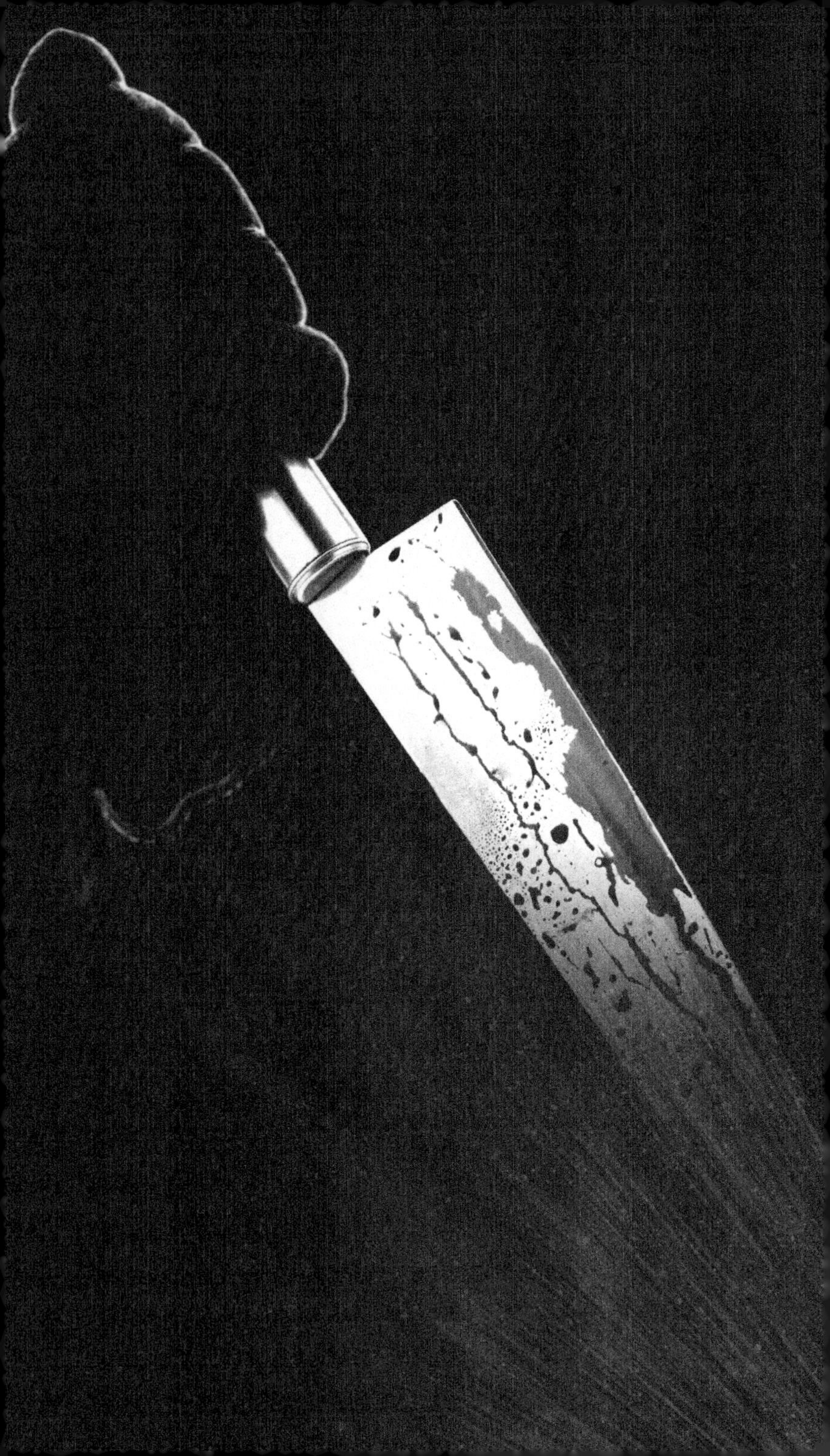

CHAPTER 24
DARIA

It's only a few days before Halloween, and I'm getting twitchy. I want this to be over with so that Mel can finally feel safe. I know she feels safe around Dad and I, but she still doesn't want to go anywhere alone. I don't blame her, but I don't have to like it either.

I want the woman I love to feel safe again, but I know that won't happen until everyone involved in her pain has been taken care of. Even then, I'm sure it will take time for her to be stop having a panic attack at the idea of being alone.

The self-defence lessons help, too. I can see her confidence coming back with every lesson, and it's beautiful to watch.

"Mel, baby, we're going to be late," I say, walking

into the bathroom to check on her. She's been in the shower for a while.

"What?" she asks, her head under the water as she rinses her hair.

I bite my lip, looking over her curvaceous body as the water covers every inch of her skin. By the time my eyes catch that sweet ass of hers, I'm horny as fuck.

Stripping my clothes off, I decide we can be a few minutes late. I need to taste her. "Nothing," I reply when I open the door.

"Frig!" she screeches, whirling around to face me. "You scared the crap out of me, Dari!"

I smirk, moving under the water with her and gently pushing her against the wall. "Sorry?"

She scoffs but smiles at me, her eyes lighting up when I look at her lips. "What are you doing in my shower, Dari? We're going to be late," she says, and the irony of me coming in to tell her that isn't lost on me. But like I said, I'm fine with taking a few minutes in order to have her falling apart on my tongue.

"My woman needs to cum," I say, kissing her neck. "I think we can spare a few minutes. Don't you?"

"Just me?" she moans, lifting her chin to give me better access to her throat. "That doesn't seem very fair." She's already breathless and needy, and I fucking love it.

"I'm not the one wound up tighter than an eight-day-alarm-clock, Mel." I nip her throat, letting my hands travel down her body and stopping to cup her breasts.

"I'm fine," she groans, and I pinch her nipple until she's squirming.

"No lies, baby. I can read you like a book."

I move to kiss her, loving how she instantly opens up for me.

The second our tongues graze, I kiss her harder, ravishing her mouth and moving my hand down to her centre, moaning into her when I feel how slick she is for me.

"God, baby. You get so wet for me." I nip her lip and stroke her clit with the pad of my finger.

"I'm in the shower, Dari," she says breathlessly, refusing to let go of her sass.

"Oh, baby, we both know that's not what's causing you to squirm." I chuckle against her neck.

Dipping down, I take a nipple into my mouth, sucking and biting until her whimpers are echoing around the shower before dropping to my knees.

"Daria," she whines, her hands going to my hair, and I smirk.

"Are you going to let me eat you out? I'm hungry, Mel."

I watch her swallow and nod her head, and fuck, her submission makes me more desperate to take her.

"Try and keep it down. We don't want Dad running in here." I smirk at her, and she blushes like crazy. I know she can't hold back her screams, but it's fun to watch her try.

Lifting her leg over my shoulder, I kiss her thigh and drag my lips up until I can bite down on the junction of her thighs, making her whimper and grind her pussy against the corner of my mouth.

"Daria, please," she begs, and I know she needs this.

"Anything for you, Mel." I mean every word.

She's not only anxious about Halloween, but the fact that her dad is flying in today. She's terrified he'll figure something out, but he won't. Dad and I are too good at hiding in plain sight, and we respect her wishes that Mr. Mahone never knows we're killers.

I run my nose along her folds, breathing in her sweet scent and teasing her clit before nipping it with my teeth, making her shiver.

"My pussy," I growl against her, making sure she feels the vibrations before flicking my tongue against her clit.

"Oh, God," she moans, her hands moving into my hair and pushing my face harder against her.

Flattening my tongue, I lick her sweet cunt, devouring the taste of her. I know we don't have a lot of time, so I move my fingers to her entrance. Lifting my eyes to watch her reaction, I slam two of them into her.

"Jesus!" she cries out as I start fucking her with my fingers and tongue in tandem.

I love the feel of her clenching around my fingers as I bring her closer and closer to the edge.

"God, I love you, Mel," I growl against her clit before pulling my fingers out of her sweet cunt.

"I love you, too," she whimpers, hating the loss of my fingers inside of her.

But she shouldn't fret. I move my fingers to her ass and press one against her hole while attacking her clit with my tongue.

"Oh, fuck. Shit," she moans as I slowly dip my fingertip in and out of her ass while tonguing her clit. I love how she loses her sweetness and starts cursing when she's like this.

When she's squeezing down on my finger, whimpering and pulling at me hair painfully, I move my other hand between us to strum her clit while dragging my tongue to her entrance.

"Cum for me, Melanie. Cum so hard the whole

goddamn building knows who the fuck you belong to." I thrust my tongue into her pussy, pushing my finger deeper and faster into her back entrance until she's flooding my face with her release.

"Fucking, shit! Goddamn, Daria. Yesssssss!" she screams, grinding her cunt into my face as I drink down her release like the greedy bitch I am.

I discovered just how much Melanie loved her ass being played with last week when we were exploring, and now I do it every chance I get because she's a squirter when I fuck all of her holes with no mercy.

Her knees buckle above me, and I catch her before she falls. Dropping her leg off my shoulder, I chuckle as I stand and help her back to her feet.

"God, you're beautiful when you fall apart," I whisper, kissing her gently until she's once again steady on her feet.

"You're going to kill me one of these days," she groans, but she's smiling, and the tension has eased in her body, so I'll count it as a win.

"Never." I nip at her chin playfully. "But we really are going to be late if we don't get our asses out of this shower," I tell her, and she laughs.

"Yeah, you think?" She wraps her arms around my neck and kisses me gently before laying her head on my shoulder. "I love you, Dari. I don't know how I'd have survived all of this without you by my side."

My heart constricts in my chest as I hug her back, kissing the side of her head. I move one hand to shut the shower off before giving her a final squeeze and pulling back.

"You would have because you're stronger than you fucking realize," I tell her. "But you never have to find out because I'm not going anywhere, baby."

Even if she asked me to step away from her, I'd still watch over her from a distance like a dark guardian angel because she has my whole heart and always will.

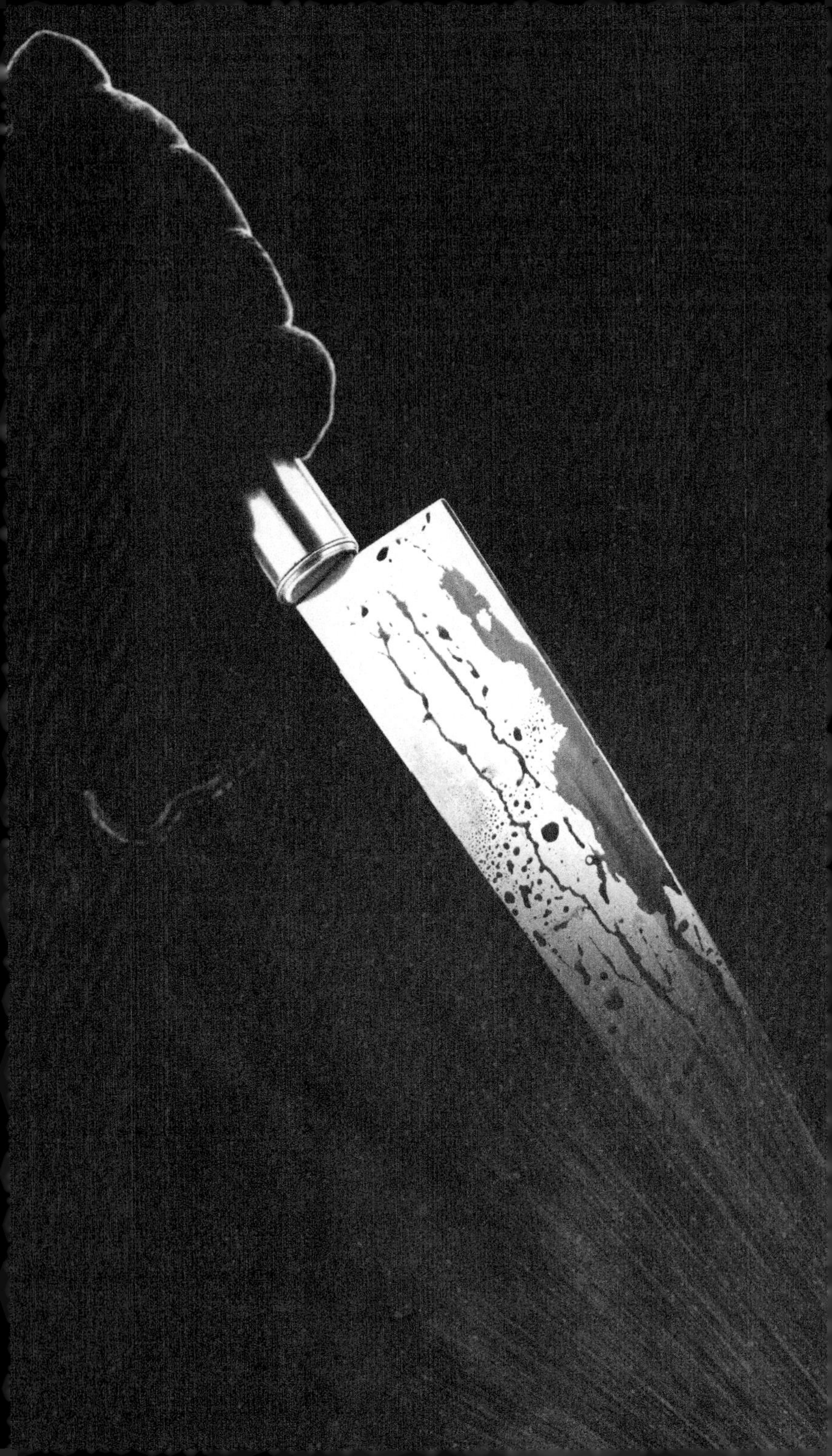

CHAPTER 25
MELANIE

It's a really good thing Dad loves me, because we were definitely late to pick him up. Between our extra-curricular activities in the shower and traffic, he was waiting for us for over an hour, and he wasn't very happy about it.

"Daria's father lives here?" Dad asks in disbelief.

I try my best not to wince because he's never been all that soft spoken about people who make a show of having money. Not that that's what Kane is doing with this apartment, but Dad can't know why it's so important to have this type of security. Being the head of a company wouldn't be reason enough for him.

At least he won't be meeting Kane, so it's only me and Daria that have to navigate this situation.

"Um, sometimes, yeah," I tell him.

I quickly get the door unlocked and usher Dad in before closing it and locking the place back up.

"Sometimes?" he barks, not trying to be rude. He's just shocked I think.

"He travels a lot." It's all I'm willing to tell him at the moment.

"Right. I suppose as the head of a large company such as his, he would need to travel more often than not."

"Yeah, but Daria and I stay here. Now that we're taking classes online and working for his company, it's easier and more convenient than trying to stay in the dorms." I swallow down the bile that rises as I think about even going back to campus.

Even after they're dealt with, I'm pretty sure I'm going to have a hard time stepping foot on the property again. Some things will just always be a reminder.

"Yes," Dad says, frowning at me. "I really think you made a mistake, Melanie." He's angry. He has been from the moment I told him I switched paths, and I understand his concern.

I'm still taking all of the same courses as before, and I'm headed for the same degree. I'm just going about it in a different way. Now that he's here with me, it's time for me to explain why I've made such a drastic change.

I couldn't bring myself to tell him over the phone. How would I even go about that? I had to wait until I could see him face to face.

"Daddy," I say, my voice breaking. That has him moving from upset to concerned in a heartbeat. "There's a reason I did that. It wasn't even about the job, really, though it is an incredible opportunity." I swallow my nerves. "Kane just offered me the same thing he did Daria because he knows we didn't want to be separated."

"What do you mean? If it wasn't the internship that made you change your mind, then what was it? This isn't like you, Melanie. You have a strong head on your shoulders."

Do I? Sometimes I wonder.

"I think you need to sit down, Dad." I move over to the couch with him, trying to not let my nerves get the best of me.

Daria gave us the space we needed to talk about this. She and Kane are doing something in preparation for Halloween. I didn't ask questions, but I figure it will be the best time for me to tell Dad. It's better if we're alone for this.

"Melanie, darling, you're scaring me," Dad whispers, and I wish I could console him.

Shaking, I take his hands in mine, trying to hold back the tears. "There's nothing to be afraid of. I'm not sick like Mom was. But something did happen to me that made... made it impossible for me to go back to campus," I push out, my voice breaking in the middle. This isn't going to be an easy conversation.

"You're not sick?"

"No, Daddy," I whisper as the first tear escapes, and sliding down my cheek.

Dad's eyes track it before he brings them back up to look at me. "What happened, Mel?"

I close my eyes and take a deep breath, trying to find that bravery inside of me. I need it so I don't move backward in my healing. I've come too freaking far for that.

"The girls at Mom's sorority didn't like me," I whisper. "They didn't want me there, and the girl... that part doesn't matter, actually." My tears are already falling, and Dad is crying right along with me.

He may not know what happened to me yet, but he can assume it isn't good if it's making me this vulnerable.

"Tell me what happened, Melanie. Please." His voice breaks, and I cry out. His pain is making this even worse. I don't want to hurt him.

"I—I was raped, Daddy," I cry, and he gasps, his body shaking.

"No!" he bellows, pulling me into his arms and

crushing me against his chest. "No. No, not my little girl."

His sadness for me is gut-wrenching, especially when it's compounded with my own, and I just hold onto him as we both cry. For a while, our cries are the only sound that can be heard through the entire apartment.

He pulls back to look at me with a tear-stained face, even as fresh ones continue to fall.

"Why didn't you come home?" he sobs, and I shake my head.

"Because it wasn't just me they hurt. Th—three guys attacked and drugged Daria in an alley the same night," I explain through my own tears. I'm not even sure my words can be understood, but I keep going. "Sh—she was able to call her dad for help before she passed out, but... I had to be with her. She's the reason I'm even functioning right now."

Dad's face is thunderous, but not in the same way Kane's is whenever he thinks about that night. No, where Kane looks lethal and deadly, Dad just looks broken and furious. Angry.

"How could this even happen?" He's not even looking at me as he tries to make sense of this. While his eyes are on me, his mind is searching for some reasonable explanation to why that night happened to either of us, but he won't find it.

Nothing about that night was reasonable.

"I couldn't tell you until I saw you face to face," I whisper. "I knew that if I had told you on the phone, you would have demanded I come home, and I needed time to recover and think." He looks pained. "I needed to be with Daria so we could work on healing together."

It's a half truth. While Daria is helping me heal and even getting revenge for us both, she hasn't struggled the way I have. She's excellent at compartmentalizing and was trained by Kane to focus her energy and upset in a much more lethal way.

We process things so differently. In fact, if their plans had been successful and they'd succeeded in raping Daria, she wouldn't have shut down like I did. She hasn't said anything, but I think her killing three guys that night is evidence enough.

Daria would have gone to the opposite extreme. She would have done the only thing she knew to do in order to feel safe.

Kill.

There would have been a trail of dead bodies behind her. One much longer than the one her and Kane will leave on Halloween.

"I understand that, Melanie. I just feel so Goddamn useless," Dad cries, pulling me into another hug. "My baby was hurt and violated, and I couldn't do anything to help her."

"I'm sorry, Daddy. I really am," I whisper, and he shakes his head in the crook of my neck.

"Please tell me you pressed charges," he demands, pulling away from me.

I suck in a breath because this is the part I was dreading the most after telling him what happened to me. I have to tell him a carefully veiled lie that will appease his anger yet not give anything away as to what truly happened or what will happen.

"Daria's Dad is working on it. But some of the people responsible have already left the school." I swallow my nerves, trying to still my shaking hands. "He thinks the others will be out before long, too, but I didn't press charges."

"Why the hell not?!" He shoots off the couch to start pacing, and I stand to stop him.

"Because I can't live through the trial and reminders, Dad. I can't do that. Please understand that would be too hard for me, but they are paying for what they've done. Kane has made sure of that," I explain, my voice steady for the first time since this conversation started.

Dad stops and searches my eyes, his pain for me so clear that it breaks my chest wide open.

"I would never want to put you through something to hurt you more, but they need to pay for what they did."

I nod, giving him another hug. "They are and will. I promise you."

He sighs, crushing me against him again as his whole body shakes from the anger and turmoil he's feeling on my behalf.

"Good. They fucking deserve whatever they get."

I wonder if he'd feel that way if he knew the truth of how they were going to pay…

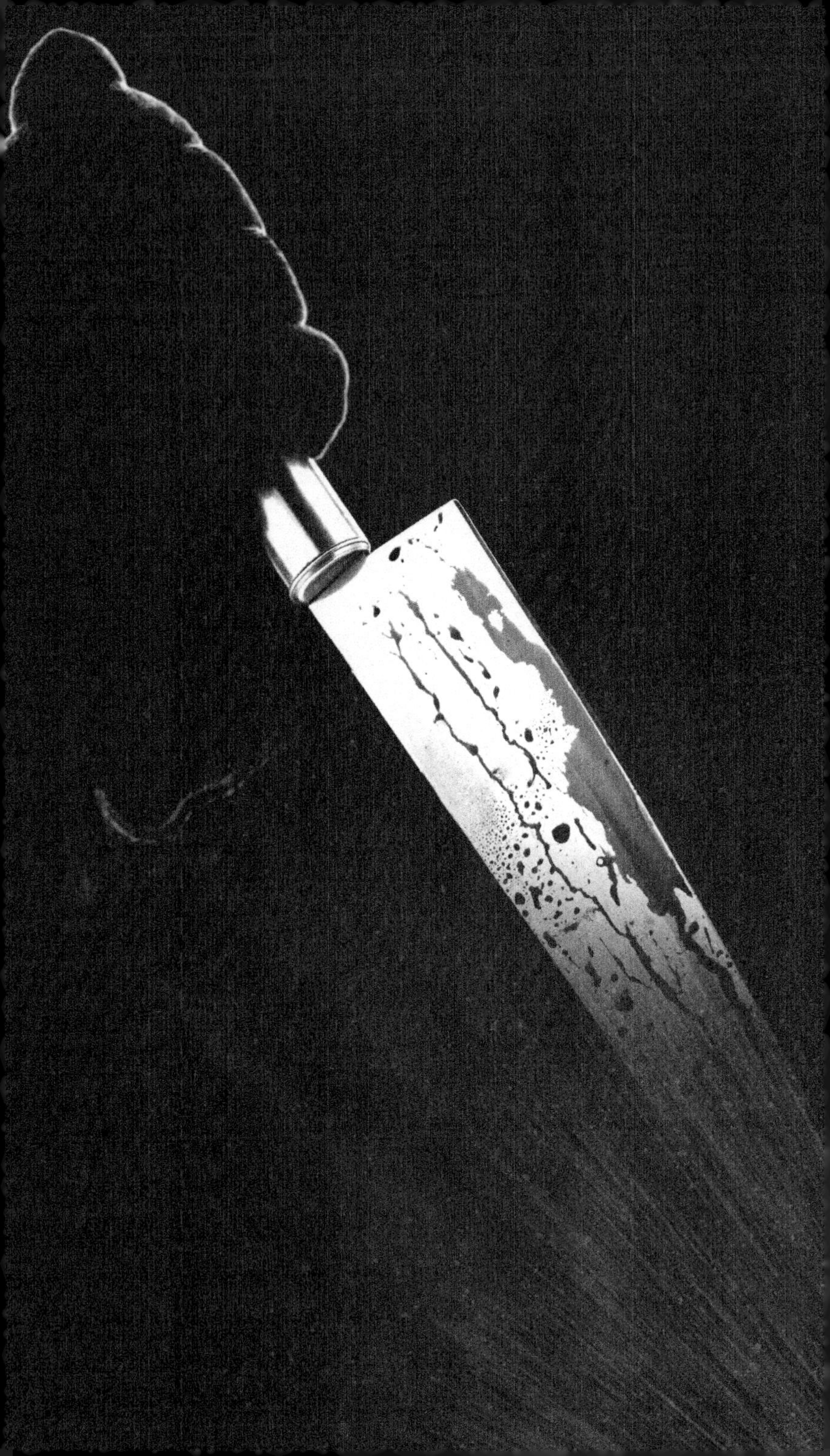

CHAPTER 26
DARIA

Dad is my hero. Honest to fuck, I want to know all of his tricks, secrets, and contacts.

"Dad, there's enough gas here to kill an army," I say in awe.

He shrugs. "Most of it is nitrous oxide to make them delirious and hallucinate first. Enough of it will cause them to have a hard time breathing. After they suffer for several minutes, then this will shut their nervous systems down." He holds up a small vial, and I beam at him.

"Sarin. I can't believe you were able to get it so quickly." Though, being who he is, he's made a lot of connections over the years. Getting a small amount of sarin gas that's untraceable probably isn't even a difficult task for him.

My fucking hero.

"I made a few calls." He smirks at me. "I'll help you make these connections, don't worry," he says, and I want to scream from excitement.

"We'll have to cover it up with a fire afterward," I say, thinking out loud. We've been over the plan dozens of times already, so he knows this.

"That'll be easy. We'll fix it to look like they were partying here. Drugs, alcohol, a fire pit. No one will question how six teenagers wound up dead on Halloween night."

I nod, looking down at the canisters of nitrous oxide. That should be a trip for them, and not the fun kind.

"I'm assuming you still want to be with me when I kill Matt and Deedra?" I ask him, and he nods.

"Yes. I just want to make sure you're alright. The sooner we take care of the bodies after you're done with them, the better." He gives me a knowing look. "I won't be in the room with you, but I want to be close by. I want to watch you work." Meaning he'll have a secured camera feed in there with me.

"You want to watch me torture them before my final kill plan?"

"Considering you refuse to tell me those final plans, yes. Besides, you won't do anything I won't be proud of you for. A father can praise his child, right?"

I cackle, bending down to hold my stomach. "Sure. Most parents praise their children for good grades or awards, but that's not our style. You praising me on my kill technique, however, feels appropriate for us."

He chuckles, shaking his head as Carlos snorts by the door.

Dude should be used to us by now.

"Do you think they've had enough time to talk?" Dad asks, turning the conversation to more serious matters.

"I think even if she has told him, they'll need some more time. Unlike you, he's a normal dad. He's not going to turn cold and calculated with rage the way you would. He's going to lose his shit," I explain, and he sighs.

"I lost my shit, too, Daria."

"I know you did. I know it was hard for you and still is, but I'm okay. I just want them to suffer. I want Mel to feel safe in her own skin again."

"He's good to her, right?" he asks me, and I blink up at him.

"Mr. Mahone? Yes, of course he is. You know that. Besides, even if he weren't the best father to her, which he is, you can't kill the only parent my girlfriend has left." I stare him down.

"I just wanted to know if I could trust him with

her in the state she's in. She's still fragile," he reminds me, like I don't know this first-hand.

"She's in perfectly good hands. He would never make this harder for her. It's sweet that you care about her so much, though."

He looks at me like I'm daft for thinking anything else. "You love her. You made the conscious choice to bring her into our family knowing what we do is dangerous. I'm not going to turn my nose up at her when she's someone you love."

Aww, my heart.

"I do love her. Don't worry, though. I doubt I will ever have feelings for anyone else I meet."

He smiles. "You are way too much like me, kid."

I am. I'm his mini replica as far as attitude and behaviour goes. But looks wise? I'm all Mom, and I think he curses that often, too.

"I'm not all you. I have Mom's stubbornness on top of yours. And I look like Mom," I tease, and he scowls.

Mom is hot. Not in a weird way, but in an objective, I can take a step back and realize that, kind of way.

"Yes, you do. I'm amazed I haven't had to kill more men for traipsing after you."

I gape at him. "What do you mean *more* men?!"

Carlos laughs from the door. "You mean she doesn't know?" he says to Dad, laughing harder.

Dad scowls at him. "Why the fuck would I tell her that?" He focuses back on me. "There may have been a few… strays I've disposed of over the years."

What?

"Dad."

"It's not like you ever would have known who they were. They didn't outright make a move on you, but given the fact you are beautiful like your mother, there have been men that have made passing comments about you that I didn't approve of." He shrugs like it's not a big deal.

"How many is a few?" I ask because, it may not be a huge deal to him, but it's something I think I would have liked to know.

"Two or three."

Carlos coughs out *LIAR* and Dad sighs.

"Fine. Six."

Now that's just not fair. I could have been helping him kill people sooner, or at least been a part of it.

"Okay. I'm not upset that you killed them if they made obscene comments about me. I trust your judgement. But really? You couldn't have at least let me be a part of those kills? They were about me, after all."

"Daria, if I had let you start watching kills when

you were fifteen, your mother would have murdered me."

"Gross! Fifteen? I hope they died horribly slow, and painfully." I gag at the thought of men making sexual comments about me at that age. Some people are just fucking disgusting.

A dark look washes over his face as he smiles. "Oh, trust me, sweetheart. It was a pleasure."

Yeah, see? He's always going to be my hero.

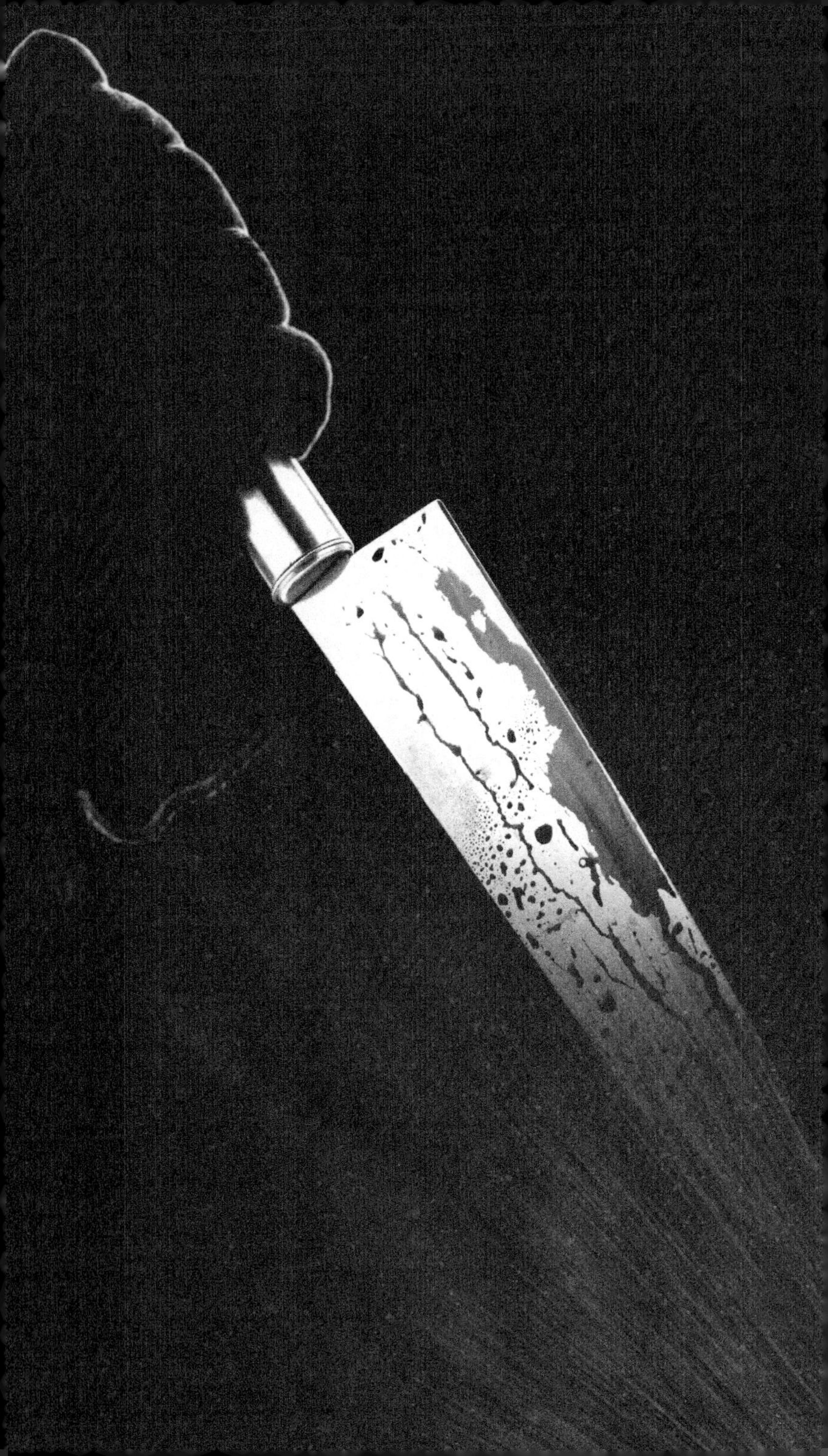

CHAPTER 27
MELANIE

The moment Daria closes our bedroom door, I'm awake.

I've gotten used to sleeping with her by my side, so not having her here makes it harder. The nightmares tend to come back when she's not with me.

"How did it go?" I ask as she strips down to her panties and tosses a t-shirt over herself before climbing into bed.

"Excellent," she says with a snicker, and I roll my eyes in the dark.

Honestly, I should probably be concerned with how excited the woman I love gets over death and destruction, but I can't bring myself to care. Not when I know she's doing it for the right reasons. It's not like she's going out and killing random people for absolutely no reason.

"How did things go with your dad?" she asks gently pulling me into her arms.

"Okay, I guess. He's not thrilled that I didn't go to the police, and he's angry that it happened to me at all." My voice breaks as I fight the emotions that have been trying to pull me under all night.

"Hey, it's okay, baby. We don't have to talk about it. Are you okay?" she asks gently, and I nod.

"Yeah, Dari, I'm fine. It was just hard to see Dad like that, you know?"

She sighs, kissing my head. "I get that. It wasn't even easy for me to tell Dad what they tried to do to me, and he's not nearly as emotional as Mr. Mahone."

I chuckle, knowing she's right. "Oh, he's emotional, he's just deadly and lethal rather than having a normal reaction."

"Yeah, you're right. The day he dropped me off on campus, he told me if something ever happened to me, he'd destroy everyone involved before burning the world to the ground and taking himself out." She's quiet for a second. "Never mind. He's over emotional. Don't tell him I said that, though."

I laugh and shake my head, loving how easily she can bring me back to the present moment. "Your secret is safe with me, promise," I smart off, laughing when she snorts at me.

"What are you and Mr. Mahone doing for Halloween?" she asks me, and I shrug.

"I figured we would stay in and watch movies. I also plan on discreetly getting drunk so he can't see how shot my nerves are while I wait to hear from you."

"Mel, have you ever been drunk in your life?" she asks me, a teasing note to her voice.

"Uh, no." I wince.

She starts laughing and pressing kisses down my face and neck.

"Then he's going to know you're drunk."

She's not wrong. I'm sure I'm a completely different person when I'm drunk. "Fine. I'll make him watch absolutely terrifying horror movies so I have an excuse to jump at anything."

I moan when she kisses my neck and reaches down to squeeze my ass. "Besides," I breathe out, grinding my hips into her. "There's a new one coming out tomorrow, and I hear it's amazing. You know I can't miss a movie when it comes out."

"Mmm," she moans against my neck, moving back up to take my mouth with hers in a heated kiss that leaves us both breathless when she pulls back. "My sweet, adorable movie snob."

"It's not my fault that I enjoy getting lost in a good movie. And the ratings on this one from theatre-goers is actually fantastic, so sue me," I say sternly, making her chuckle.

"I love when you get all hot and nerdy about these things, you know," she teases, and I laugh with her.

"I'm glad my nerdiness has its benefits in our relationship."

"Anything you use that tongue for is hot," she whispers against my mouth.

"That was the cheesiest shit you've ever said to me," I tease before taking her mouth with mine and rolling her onto her back. "But it worked, and I owe you an orgasm after this morning." I nip her lip, grinding my pelvis into hers. "You denied me your pussy, Dari. I'm very sad about that."

"Are you?" she breathes out, lifting her hips into me. "Then do something about it, Mel. No one is stopping you now." She smirks at me, taunting me to take her.

"Game on, babe. Hands above your head and don't move them. If you do, I'll have to stop and tie them behind your back."

Her eyes flare at my order. She loves when I take a dominant stance with her. I have no idea where this side of me came from, either, but it's clear she woke something inside of me that was lying dormant.

I watch Daria raise her hands over her head like I

asked, then smile down at her, lifting her shirt up until it's rolled into a gag over her mouth. "Open up, Dari. You can't be loud tonight, and I have plans for you."

She groans but opens her mouth, letting me place it securely.

Bending down, I take her nipple into my mouth and suck, loving the muffled moans already coming from her.

Once I have the peak stiff and wet, I pull off and gently blow cold air onto it, smirking when she throws her head back. Then move to give the other one the same attention until she's squirming under me.

"I love your boobs, Dari," I praise, giving it one last nip with my teeth. "But I think you want my mouth somewhere else."

"Ahhgrh!" she whimpers against the shirt.

Chuckling against her skin, I drag my tongue down her body until I reach the waistband of the lace panties she has on. Using my teeth, I nibble across the panty line, loving how easily I can smell her arousal from here.

"God, babe. You smell so good. I bet you're soaked for me," I whisper, moving to pull the scrap of lace down her legs and tossing them on the floor beside us.

"I love how hot you get for me, Dari," I moan.

She's already spread her legs to show me just how badly she wants me, and I'm almost ready to just fuck her and be done with it. But I can't. I wasn't kidding when I said I was sad she denied me this morning.

I love that I'm one of two women that have ever gone down on her. She told me after the first time we were together that the first one had been when she was sixteen, and it wasn't anything like how I make her feel.

"Goddamn, babe," I whimper. I quickly rip my shirt and underwear off before laying on my stomach between her thighs.

"Mine." It's all the warning she gets before I start teasing her clit with my tongue.

Daria is moaning and grinding her hips against me in no time, and I'm desperate to make her cum for me.

I move my fingers to her entrance and slowly slide two inside, pumping them slow and deep until she's crying out against the shirt, begging me to take her over that edge.

"Hold still, babe," I warn her before pulling my fingers out and coating my pinky in her juices.

Moving my two fingers back into her pussy, I slide my pinky to her back entrance and slowly press it in, watching as she throws her head back in pure delight.

I'm not the only one who loves having their ass played with.

I focus my mouth back on her clit, fucking her holes with my fingers in a steady rhythm until she's screaming her release. She's bearing down on my fingers and screaming as I lap up every drop she gives me.

Gently, I pull my fingers from her before moving up the bed and pulling her shirt out of her mouth. The second it's out, she whips it off her head and tackles me to the bed, kissing me furiously and straddling my hips to grind down on me.

"My turn to make you cum, Mel. I'm going to fuck you senseless, and you have to be quiet," she growls against my mouth before moving her hand to cover it.

"Ohh," I scream against her hand as she starts rolling her hips against mine.

The way her pussy drags over mine—up and down, circle, repeat—drives me wild. Our combined slickness makes it easy for Daria to fuck me hard and raw while I'm fully surrendered to her, and I can't breathe through the pleasure.

"Fuck, baby. You feel so goddamn good. My precious girl, letting me fuck her hard. You need this, don't you, Mel?" she moans, bucking against me harder until I'm screaming against her hand and blacking out from the pleasure taking over my body.

When I start to come back down, I feel Daria cleaning me up with a warm cloth. Once she's finished, she climbs back onto the bed and leans over me to kiss me gently.

"I was not expecting fierce Mel to come out and play tonight," Dari whispers with a smirk. "Gotta say, though. I'm not upset about it."

She's still breathing heavy as we both laugh a little before she drops to the bed beside me.

I roll onto my side and rest my head on her chest, catching my breath and listening to the sound of her heartbeat against my ear.

"You came too, right?" I ask after a few minutes, and she barks out a laugh.

"Yeah, baby, I came the second I saw how fucking blissed out you were. Try not to black out on me again, okay?"

I laugh, nuzzling in closer to her and closing my eyes. "Can't make any promises when you fuck me like that, Dari. That was the hottest sex I've ever had." It's an admission I don't mind making to her, and she sighs contentedly.

"It will always be amazing with us, Mel."

"Mmmm. Always."

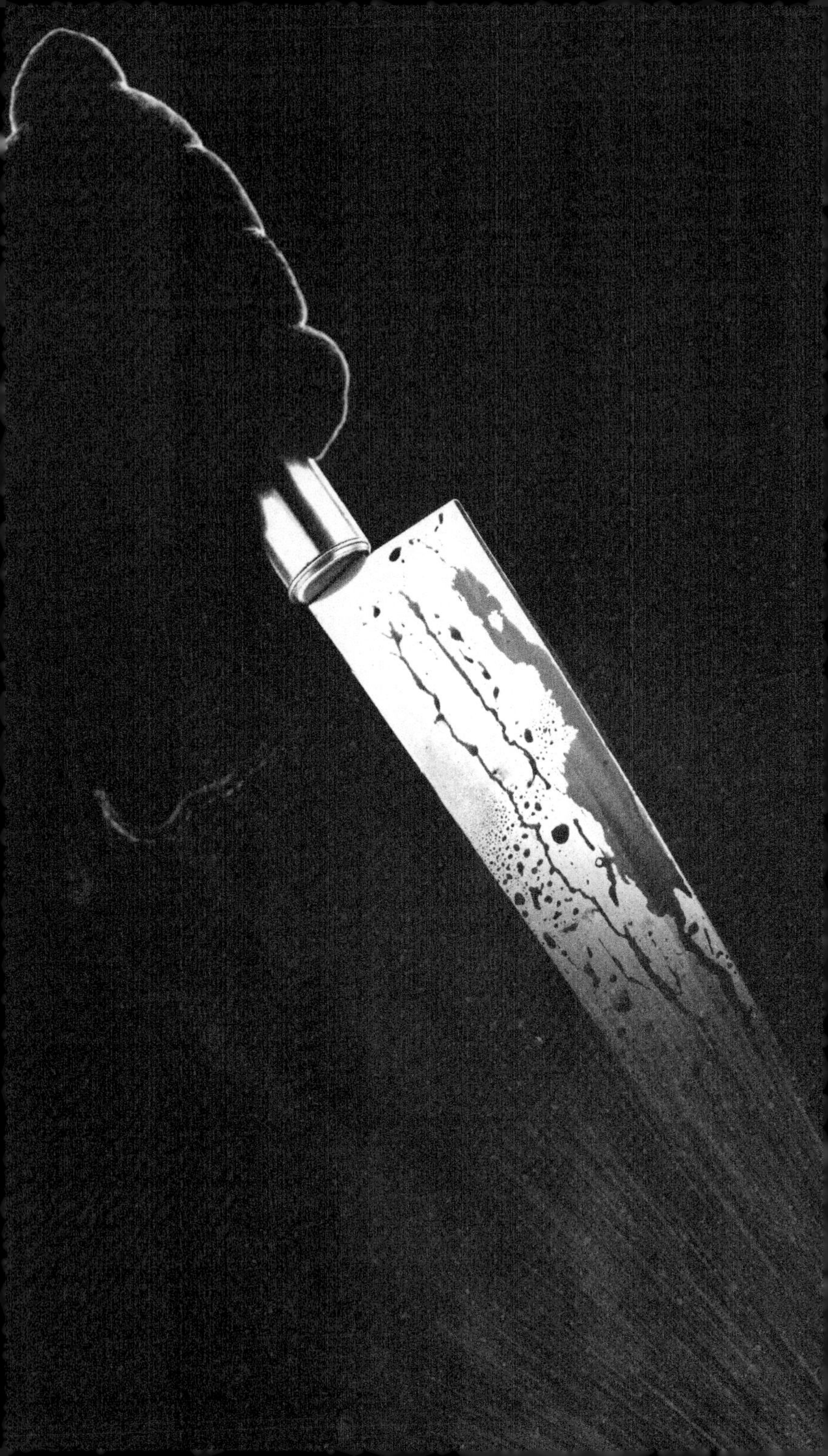

CHAPTER 28
DARIA

Their blood will run.

SCUMBAG:
Can't w8t to see you bby.

Their blood will run.

SCUMBAG:
What are you dressing as? Let me guess… sexy nurse?

ME:
Mmm, horror movie victim. You know the ones? They're all slutty and covered in blood?

SCUMBAG:
Fuck yeah! Hot tits bouncing and shit. Fuck, I'm hard 4u.

Their blood will run.

If I keep reminding myself I'm only hours away from killing him, maybe I won't barf.

> ME:
> Yeah? Should I wear a blonde wig or red? I want you to decide.

> SCUMBAG:
> Blonde bby. Redheads are fuck toys. You're more than that 2 me.

Fuck. Nope.
Their blood will run.

> ME:
> Hehe okay, yay! I have to clock back in for work, but I'll see you tonight! Excited to meet you finally.

"More like, excited to destroy you. But, potato potatoe."

"Fuck, sweetheart. You need to wipe the murder off of your face before Mel gets back from lunch with her dad," Dad grunts at me, shaking his head.

"Would you like to take over flirting with this fucker, then? Because he just told me to wear a blonde wig because redheads are fuck toys, and I mean more to him than that," I state, glowering at the burner phone when it goes off again.

SCUMBAG:

3 hours bby. Be ready.

"Oh, and that I should be ready for him in three hours."

Dad sneers. "You are ready for him in three hours, but if he thinks he's getting lucky, he's going to whine like a little bitch when you tie him up."

I hum with happiness and pocket the burner phone. "Oh, I guarantee he will whine like the little bitch he really is by the time I'm finished with him," I tell Dad, and he smiles at me proudly.

"That's my girl. Now, let's get this meeting over with so we can get to the real fun." He winks at me, and I laugh.

"Let the games begin."

The music is already blaring from inside the old church, and Carlos is standing as the fake security at the door as each of them shows him their ID one by one before being let into the 'exclusive party'.

Just as I figured they would, Matt and Deedra choose to be the last ones to enter, which makes grabbing them so much simpler than it could have been.

We had plans for every situation, but this is the best outcome for the quickest results.

ME:

> I love you, Mel. Talk to you in a while.

I shoot the text off to Melanie before putting it on silent so I can join Dad in watching Carlos quickly drug the other two without issue.

Deedra is so caught up with trying to get into his pants while Matt stares at his phone, they don't even see it coming.

"It's time. Are you ready?" Dad turns to ask me. I don't even dignify that with a response before heading toward the church.

Now that Carlos has locked the only door in and out of the building that wasn't previously secured, we can administer the gas into the air with the balloons.

"Oh, they're freaking out," Carlos sings out at the sounds of screaming and pounding against the door and windows surround us.

The windows were already barred before Dad found the place. I don't know what type of church in the middle of nowhere would need bars on the windows, but they make our job easier tonight.

"They're about to freak out even more." I snicker, grabbing the trigger Dad hands me. "Three. Two.

One." I hit the button and watch on the camera as several of the balloons break in tandem, causing mass hysteria inside the church.

"How long until the nitrous oxide takes effect?" Carlos asks as we all watch the camera feed in fascination.

Their screams are music to my ears. They aren't nearly as satisfying as the other two's will be, but it's still lovely to hear.

"Not long. Look, the smaller of them are starting to giggle. It's already getting into their nervous system. Give it another minute or two and the six of them will start really struggling to breathe while their mind and body fight for oxygen," Dad explains.

We watch as the bigger guys start laughing and fucking around with one another as the girls begin to panic. They're beginning to realize they can't breathe properly.

Everyone has forgotten the windows now, their survival instincts slowing from the lack of oxygen to their brains.

As soon as we watch the guys realize they can't breathe and the girls fall to the ground, clutching their chests, I click the other trigger switch to release a very small amount of sarin gas into the room.

"Holy shit," Carlos comments, his eyes locked on

the screen as we watch them all take their last breaths.

"Daria, go grab the camera from outside of the window. Carlos, let's get these two tied up and gagged before they wake up," Dad gives the orders, and we all do what's needed to get this show on the road.

Once I have the camera in my hand, I walk back over to meet Dad and Carlos as Carlos gets into a hazmat suit. He's going to be the one to go inside of the church and set it on fire, making it look like an accident.

"Be careful in there, Carlos," Dad says in a gruff tone. "Make sure you're enclosed in that thing tightly."

Carlos nods while he and Dad make sure the suit is on safely before he unlocks the church door and goes inside.

"He'll check to make sure they're dead before he starts the fire."

"I know, Dad. What happens when they find no smoke in their lungs during an autopsy?" I ask him, still worried about that part.

"They won't, sweetheart. It will never be on the record. I paid good money to make sure of that," he declares, watching as smoke begins to fill the windows inside.

Carlos makes his way out of the church, stopping at the doors to strip out of his suit before tossing it into the tub of acid they have set up and stripping his clothes off as well.

Deciding I don't need to see the man naked, I move my eyes back to the church windows where I see the beginnings of an orange glow in the coming from near the old pulpit.

"Come on, Daria, let's go." Dad grabs my attention.

When I look back over at them, Carlos is getting dressed in another set of clothes, and his hair is wet where Dad doused him with water to make sure there are no traces of the gas on his body.

"Lou is coming to grab the acid. He's waiting down the road for our signal," Carlos explains once he has his body covered again.

"Good. Daria, you lie in the back until I tell you otherwise. Lou is a good man and the clean-up of acid is his bread and butter, but I don't trust him to know you exist. I don't want him to see more than me and Carlos in the SUV on the way out."

"I know the drill, Dad. Let's do this."

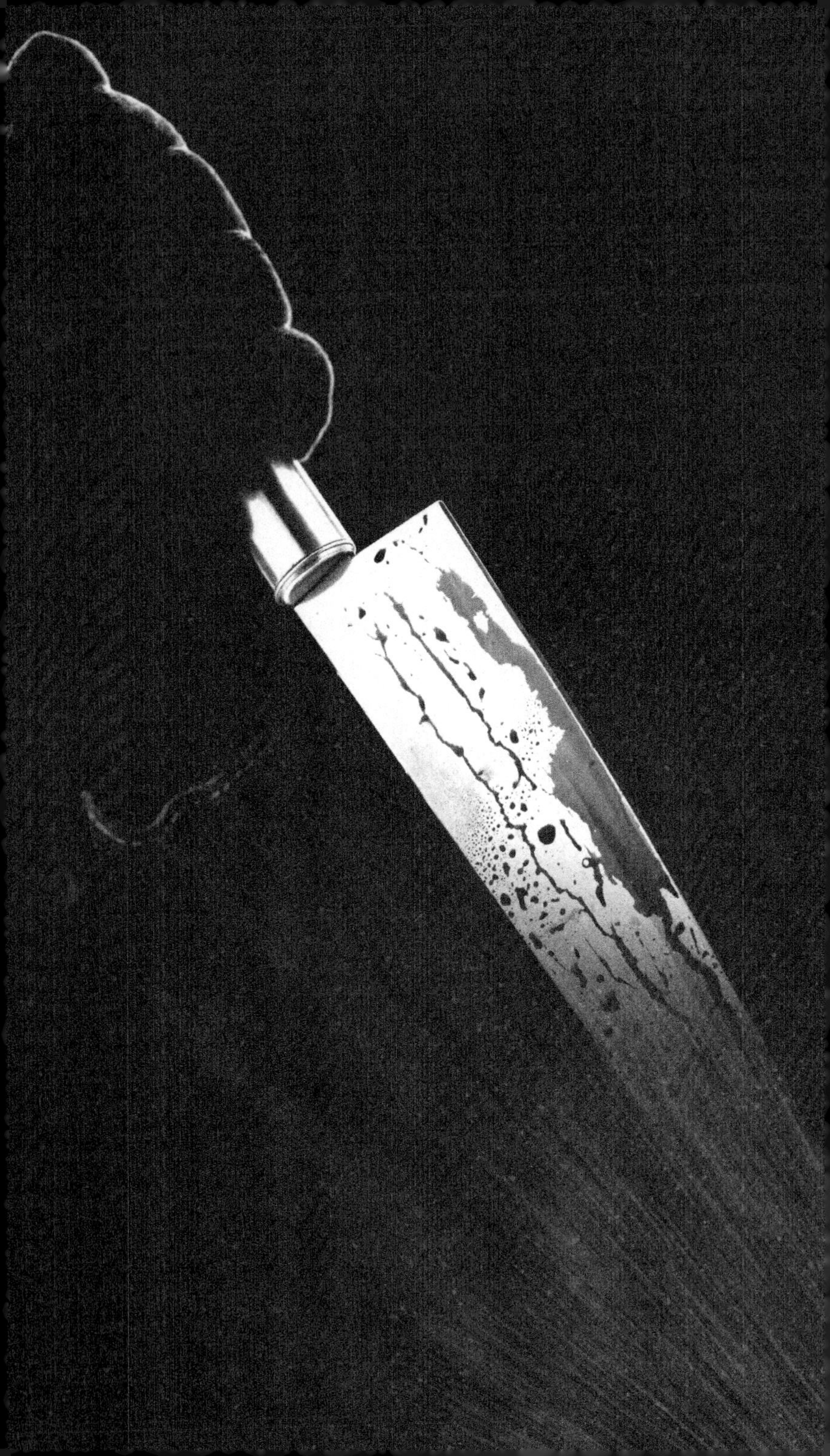

CHAPTER 29
DARIA

"Wakey, wakey," I taunt both Matt and Deedra while I wait for them to fully come out of their drugged states.

Torturing them won't be nearly as enjoyable if they aren't aware of why they're in pain.

Dad is in the other room watching over the secure camera feed, and I have to admit I'm looking forward to his thoughts on my chosen forms of torture tonight. Especially the grand finale.

"What?" Matt grumbles, stirring on the cement floor where he's chained to the wall.

We're in the basement of one of the many buildings Dad uses when he needs to torture someone before they disappear. There isn't much in this room aside from a table for the tools and equipment we choose to use and a large drain by their bodies to make clean up easier.

"Matty, look at you waking up first. Chop, chop. I wanna play!" I clap excitedly, making him jump. He groans when he tries to move his hands and can't since they're tied behind him.

"What the hell?" Deedra's voice is whiny and high pitched as she comes to, instantly grating on my nerves.

"Where are we?" Matt grumbles, his eyes opening as he starts to pull on the chains.

"You're in Hell," I tell him simply.

His eyes bounce around the room a few times before landing on me and widening. "Daria?"

"Hey, hi, it's me." I smile, walking over to him with my knife in hand.

"Where are we? And why are we tied to a wall in a cold and damp room?" he questions, his eyes erratic as they continue scanning every surface they land on.

"I told you that if I found out you'd touched her, I'd bury you. This is me fulfilling that promise," I hiss, getting in his face and holding the knife to his throat.

"What the hell are you doing?!" Deedra screeches, clearly not liking the fact I'm holding a knife to her fuck-boy's throat.

"Shut up, Pippi. I'll get to you in a second," I snap at her. "Right now, I'm letting your boy Matty here know just how badly he fucked up."

"You won't hurt me," he says with a bravado he definitely doesn't feel. I can see the fear in his eyes.

I pull back, laughing and shaking my head. I toss the knife into the air before catching it when it comes back down. Up, down. Up, down. They both track the knife as I play with it, probably wondering if I'm going to throw it at them next.

"You know that saying about being careful who you fuck with?"

He swallows and nods as Deedra screeches at us both. She's so fucking loud I can't even understand what she's saying. Not that I care.

"It was made because of people like me." I move back over and kneel in front of him, slamming my knife into his leg just above the kneecap.

His scream of pain washes over me, giving me a high I didn't get to experience with the assholes in the alleyway.

"Fuck! Cunt! Shit!" he curses, and I snort at how unoriginal he is.

Deedra is silent as she watches me rip the knife out of his leg before throwing up between them.

"Weak stomach, Pippi?" I taunt as blood darkens the jeans Matt is wearing.

"What the fuck is wrong with you?" Matt bellows in my direction, and I shrug.

"You should be asking yourself that question. How can you look at yourself in the mirror every day?" I dig my heal into his wound, making him scream in agony. "You raped my girlfriend."

"You can't rape the willing," he hisses, throwing the words at me through clenched teeth.

"The willing? She was so willing that your whore of a girlfriend had to hold her down so you could take her?" I ask, letting my anger fully wash over me.

Deedra squeaks, and I move over to kneel before her. "You are a bitch," I hiss in her face, moving the knife to her cheek. "You were horrible to Mel. Just because she's different?"

I drag the knife downward, leaving a gash on her cheek in its wake as her cries echo around the room.

They're both screaming in terror already, and I've barely gotten started. It's going to be a wonderful night.

"Where was I before I got impatient and stab-happy? Oh yeah! That saying about be careful who you fuck with? You should have heeded my warning in the cafeteria," I tell them when their cries have subsided enough for me to be heard.

"What the hell are you talking about, you stupid

cunt?!" Matt snaps at me, and the door to the room slams open.

Sighing, I watch Dad walk in, looking every bit of the deadly assassin he is.

"She's talking about me, you little twerp," Dad growls, leaning down to wrap his large hand around Matt's neck. "I'm the thing your nightmares run from, and you tried to hurt my daughter."

"Dad! Come on, you're going to kill him before I even get to play," I groan.

Matt's eyes are bulging out of his head as he looks at Dad.

"If you think she isn't a threat, think again. Did you ever wonder where your other buddies went?" I watch Matt's eyes flick to me before going back to Dad. "Yeah. She took all three of them on and killed every last one of them by herself. You aren't leaving this room alive, asshole."

Dad releases his throat and stands up, moving over beside me while Matt chokes on the air he tries to pull back into his lungs.

"Feel better?" I ask, and he smiles at me.

"Much. I'd kill him myself for even thinking about touching you, but this is your revenge. I'll leave you to it." He kisses my head before exiting the room again.

"Who are you?" Matt asks in a shaky voice, and I smile.

"I'm The Hunter's daughter."

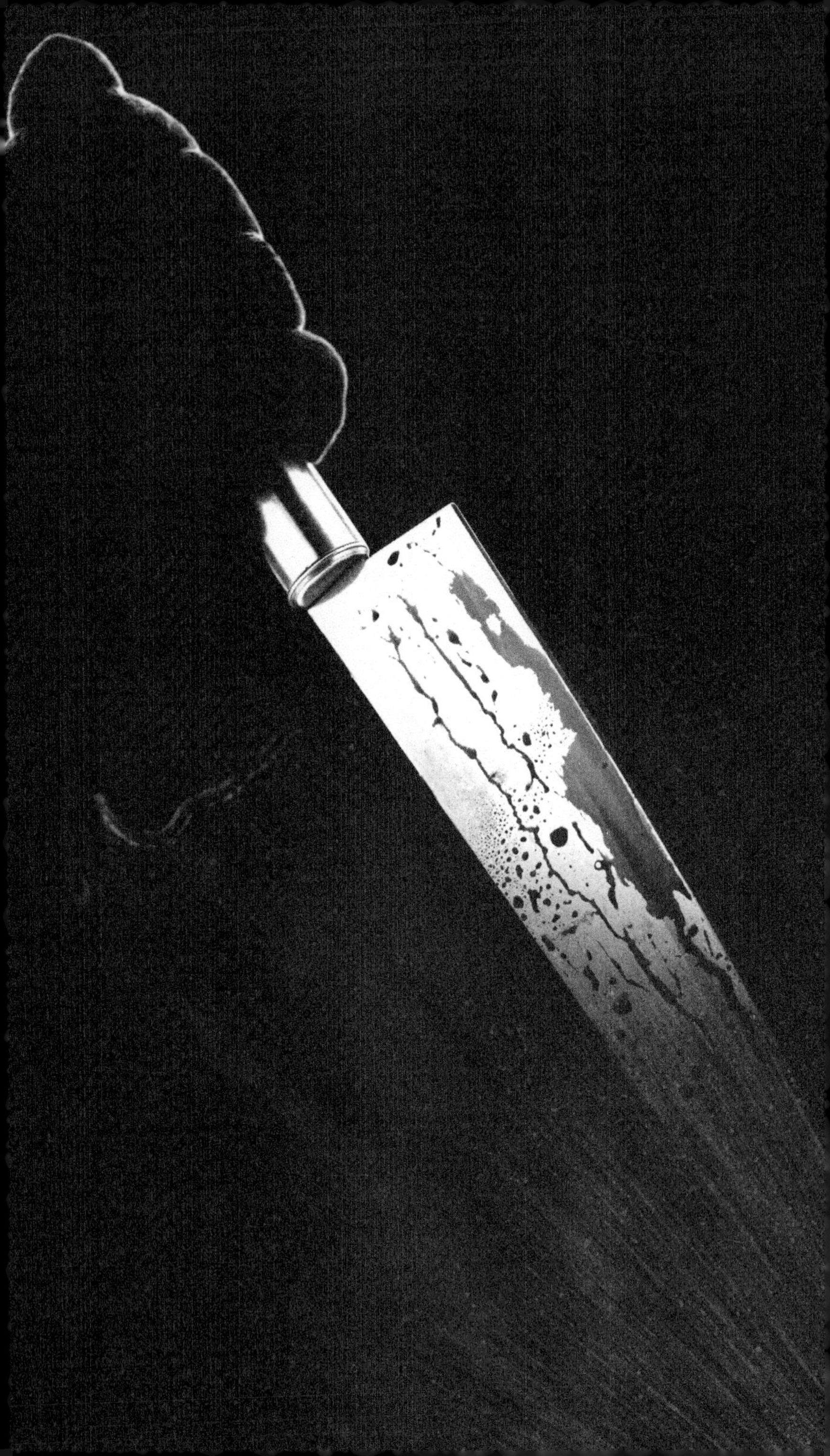

CHAPTER 30
KANE

There's instant recognition on the boy's face.

It doesn't matter if you're a good and honest person, the tales of my kills are spread far and wide, striking fear into everyone who hears them.

I've been a killer since I was seventeen years old. I don't foresee stopping any time soon, either. It's who I am down to my very DNA. One look at Daria right now is proof of that.

"Lost your shit back there," Carlos grunts when I sit back down beside him to watch Daria do her thing.

"I needed to work off some of my anger. You know she's my weakness, and they drugged and tried to rape her," I growl, watching Daria shove her knife into that little twerp's stomach.

Carlos winces, chuckling when she twists it

before pulling out and moving over to the screeching banshee beside him. That bitch seriously needs to be silenced. I can barely fucking hear myself think.

"She's stronger than you give her credit for, Kane, but I get it." He nods toward the screen, watching her with pride as well. "If Clair and I had a daughter, I'd be the same way."

It's not often Carlos mentions his wife and the fact that they never had children, but I already know the entire story. He's been my best friend since we were kids. He's the only human being I trust on this earth outside of my daughter.

"How far do you think she'll go with the screeching witch?" he questions, knowing I don't usually condone harming women and children.

That being said, Deedra is different. Daria is the one killing her, and she has a very good reason for doing so. It's not like the bitch is innocent. These two hurt our family. They need to go.

"I doubt she'll do as much damage to her as she will the boy. He's the one who harmed Melanie the most when he tried to break her," I state.

I'm so goddamn proud as I watch Daria slice into that asshole repeatedly, never hitting anything important, but he's still bleeding too much to survive without medical care.

"That girl is the definition of sweet and innocent. These pricks had no right to hurt her," he spits out.

Carlos has been helping us train Melanie in the gym and has grown to think of her as an adopted daughter, just like he feels for Daria. His fierce loyalty will always lie with our family, just as mine does with him and Clair.

I nod my head in agreement. "She's the exact opposite of Daria," I say, wincing as we watch her slowly sink the knife into the red-head's side.

"They sure are perfect for each other, though," he comments on Daria's relationship.

"I can't argue with that." And I can't. As much of a shock as it was that Daria fell hard and fast for her roommate, I can see why. There's a magnetism between them even I can't deny.

We continue to watch Daria slice into the two of them over and over, slinging vitriol their way as she works out the aggression that's been building inside of her for weeks.

Watching Melanie suffer has taken its toll on her, and I'm glad she's finally getting to release that tension.

"You love choking on his cock, right, Pippi?" Daria snarls at the sobbing mess of a woman on the floor.

"Oh no," Carlos whispers, his eyes wide as he watches the screen.

"What?" I ask, looking at him. He's not usually squeamish.

"Asking about his dick? That can't end well," he groans, and I shrug.

"You should have seen this coming. He raped the love of her life. There was never a second where I thought that she'd let him keep his dick."

"Please don't. Oh, fuck, please don't," the boy begs with as much energy as he can muster. Most of the fight has drained from him after hours of torture.

"Oh, come now, Matty. You knew I wouldn't let you keep it. Right? You hurt her with that vile thing," Daria sneers down at the offending appendage, and my stomach churns a little at what I know will happen next. Just because I'm expecting it, doesn't make it any less gross.

"I'm sorry, okay?!" he shouts. "Just don't cut my dick off, please!" he cries out.

It's actually kind of pathetic that he's begging for his dick at this point given the fact he knows he's going to die here tonight.

"You're pathetic." She laughs at him, voicing my thoughts aloud. Sometimes I'm amazed at just how connected we are, like we share the same evil brain.

"You're bleeding out, on the verge of dying, and you can still only think about your dick?"

Matthew shakes his head with a whimper. "Please, Daria," he begs.

She sighs and stands up, moving over to the girl, and we watch as the boy breathes out a sigh of relief. He thinks he's in the clear.

"You aren't much better, Pippi," Daria says, grabbing a fist of the girl's hair. "You don't like Melanie because you know she's a better person than you could ever be. You were fucking scared to lose your spot to a legacy that you deemed beneath you." Daria slams the girl's head into the wall, dazing her. "God, you're fucking pathetic."

"That had to hurt," Carlos says, looking at me. "She's doing pretty good in there."

I smirk. "Yeah, she is. A chip off the old block," I boast, beyond proud of how she's handling her first torture session.

"NOOO!" Matthew hollers, bringing our eyes back to the screen just in time to see Daria chop his dick off.

Blood is fucking everywhere, and I feel a little sick. I can't help but commiserate the bastard on a baser human level. That there is a guy's worst nightmare.

"Eyes on me, Matty. You don't want to miss the finale," Daria says in a sing-song voice.

"What is she—no..." Carlos trails off as we watch Daria shove the boy's severed appendage down the girl's throat.

"Choke on it, you fucking bitch!" she yells at her, slamming her hand over the girl's nose and mouth while the other moves to work her throat until she can't breathe.

The sounds of gagging and choking from both Matthew and Deedra can be heard through the camera while Daria cackles as they take their final breaths together.

"See you in Hell, motherfuckers."

Carlos turns to me with wide eyes, his face paler than I've ever seen it. I imagine mine looks about the same after that display.

"That may be the most fucked up thing I've ever fucking seen," he croaks, and my eyes swing back to the camera to check on Daria. "And I've been with you from the beginning."

I can't even argue with my best friend. I've been doing this for over twenty years, and I think my daughter just outdid my worst torture sessions with one brutal move.

Holy fuck. The world isn't ready for her.

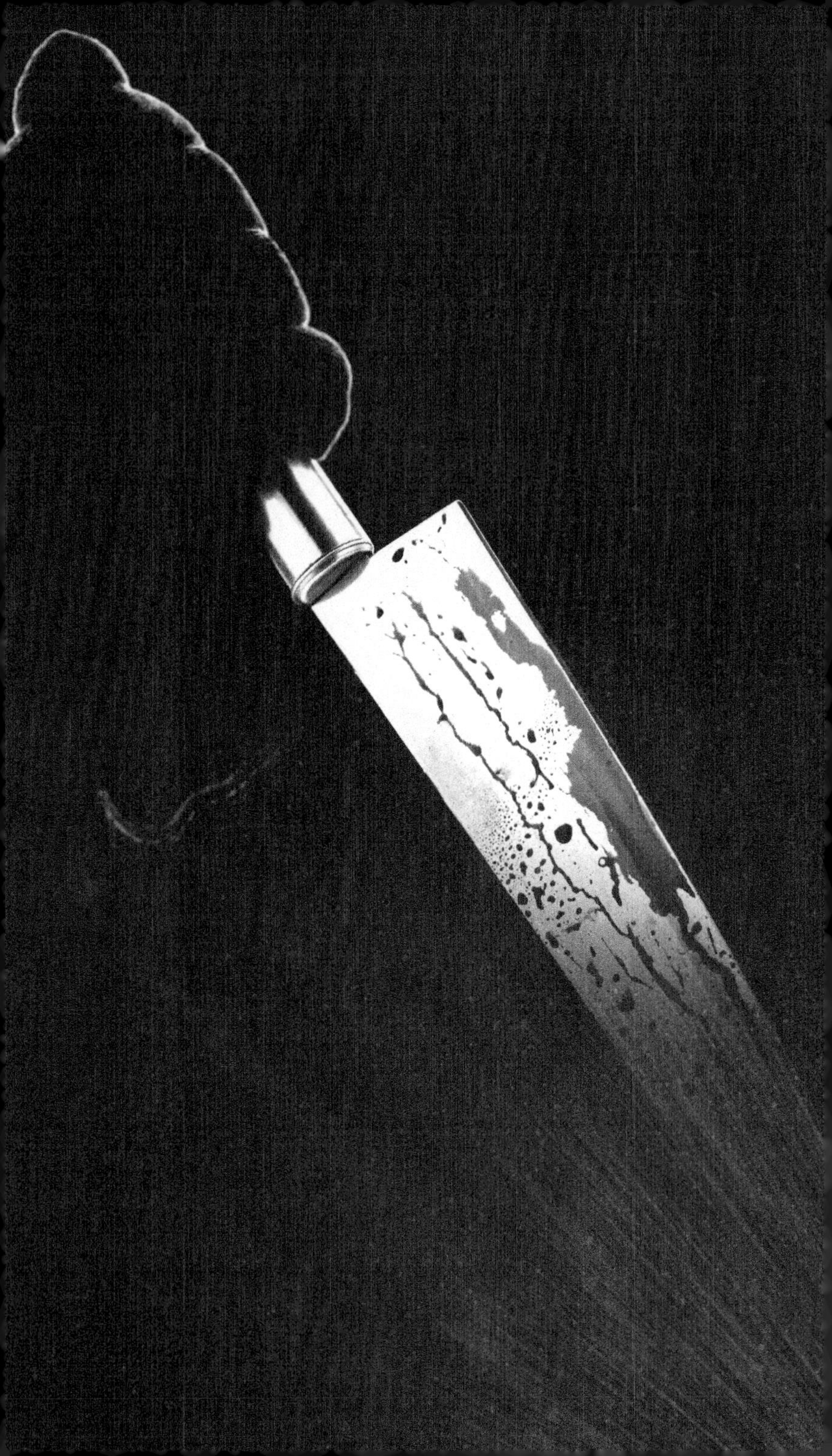

CHAPTER 31
MELANIE

I'm fairly certain Dad thinks I've lost my mind.

That horror movie may very well be the weirdest and creepiest thing I've ever seen, and that's saying something since I think I've seen them all. I never want to meet whoever decided that was a good idea to make into a movie.

Crap. I thought the opening scene of *Ghost Ship* would be the worst thing I would see in movies, but this one has it beat.

Maybe *Ghost Ship* just scarred me because I was seven when I watched it. I still remember how furious Dad was when he found me sneaking it on the tv in the middle of the night.

The door to our bedroom opens, and I jump with a shriek before realizing it's Daria.

"Shit! Are you that wound up?" Daria asks in concern, and I start laughing.

"Apparently, but it's not just you. I regret watching that movie with Dad tonight." I sit up, looking her over.

I don't know what I expected to see, but she still looks like the Daria I know and love. Nothing looks different about her, and that helps me relax. I think I thought her killing them tonight would make something change in her, but she just seems… happy.

"You scared yourself with a movie?" she asks with a smile.

"Shut up," I grumble.

Dari climbs into the bed after changing into one of her sleep shirts and pulls the covers back over our legs. "You're safe now, Mel."

Those words alone unravel a knot inside of me. I immediately start to cry, and she pulls me into her side, wrapping her arms around my shoulders so she can pat my hair in a comforting gesture.

For someone who said she wasn't good at comforting others when we first met, she's really freaking good at it with me.

"Shhh, I know, baby. I know. Let it out," she whispers, holding me close.

"I—I'm really free?" I ask her.

"You're really free, Mel. They can never hurt you or anyone else ever again."

"Thank you," I whisper, letting the tears fall as a feeling of security washes over me.

"Does it make me a bad person that I feel safer knowing they're dead?" I ask her after a while, and she snorts.

"Does it make me a bad person for wanting to make them dead so I know you're safe from your worst nightmares?" she asks back, reverse psychology at its finest.

"Never."

"Then, no. It does not make you a bad person for wanting and needing to feel safe, Melanie." She pulls back to grab my chin and look me in the eye. "I was able to give you what most victims can't. I gave you justice. I almost guarantee you that most victims of assault wish their worst nightmares would disappear. It doesn't make them bad people, either."

I blow out a breath and let her words sink in. "Yeah, I guess you're right."

"I'll never regret protecting my family, Mel," she says in a dangerously calm voice.

"I wouldn't ask you to. You may not love many, but you love fiercely. You love big when you choose to love." I shake my head with a smile. "I know you would protect us with everything you have and are, and I love you for it, Dari. Always."

"I love you, Melanie. Fucking always." Dari leans in to kiss me. "You came out of nowhere and knocked me to my knees in the best ways possible." She winks at me, making me giggle.

"I love you, Daria. I fell for you the moment you walked into our dorm room looking like a sexy badass," I tell her the same thing I always do. "You literally took my breath away. I just knew you were different."

"Right back at you, baby." She kisses me gently again, melting my heart.

The second she pulls away, she yawns, and I can see the exhaustion in her eyes. Tonight was a lot for her, but more like a cathartic experience. Now that she doesn't have to worry about their existence anymore, she's drained.

We both need some solid sleep.

"Come on, sleepyhead. Let's get some rest." I guide her to lay down and cover us with the blankets before snuggling around her and holding her close.

"Mmm, I think I like you being the big spoon," she mumbles.

"I don't mind being the big spoon sometimes. You just usually insist on being the one to hold me," I mutter back, getting comfortable.

"Safe. I need to keep you safe," she whispers before soft snores leave her. She has no clue what her words just did to me.

"You've kept me safe, Dari. Now it's my turn to protect. you."

Kissing her head, I pull her closer and fall asleep in the comfort of love and safety we've made together.

"Forever." It's a whispered promise in her sleep that I gladly respond to.

"Always."

THE END

WANT MORE?

Guess what?!

I fell in love with Kane before Chapter One was finished, and as hard as I tried to fight it, I couldn't. So... Kane is getting his own book coming Spring 2023!

What to expect:
- Age Gap
- BDSM
- Daddy/Brat dynamics (no DDlg)

PRE-ORDER HERE:

Amazon
    Apple, B&N, Kobo

CASSIE HARGROVE

Forbidden Kinks

Book 0.5:

Still His

Suited Up Daddies

1: Daddy's Naughty Secretary

2: Daddy's Little Novice

3: Daddy's Proper Present

4: Daddy's Precious Rose

5: Daddy's Sexy Sub

6: Daddy's Perfect Pair

Box Set with Bonus Novella

Serenity Stables

1: Healing with Daddy

2: A Home with Daddy

3: Rescued by Daddy

4: Protected with Daddy (Coming Nov 28/23)

Connerton Academy

(A College Paranormal Why Choose Romance)

1: Freshman Firsts

2: Sophomore Secrets

3: Junior Justice

4: Senior Sacrifices

The Revenge Diaries

(A Series of Dark/Very Dark Standalones)

1: Trick or Revenge

2: Beautiful Revenge (Original and Less Triggering Versions)

3: Love's Dark Revenge (Coming 2024)

Invisible Lines Duet

A co-write with Seven Rue

1: Blurred Lines

2: Crossed Lines

Standalones

Roommates: A Dark Sapphic Romance

The Hunter (Coming 2024)

Taboo

Depravity: An Extremely Taboo Novel (Co-Write with Seven Rue)

The Art of Freedom and Growth (A Depravity Extended Epilogue) (Co-Write with Seven Rue)

The Deadly Seven

A co-write with Story Brooks

1: Obsession

2: Seduction

3: Devotion

4: Salvation

5: Justified Retribution: Kristen's Story

Deadly Seven Omnibus (Complete Series with Bonus Scenes)

Dark Series

1: Dark Torment

2: Dark Longing

3: Dark Adoration (Coming Dec 2023)

Erotic Shorts

Taken By Him

Intern-al Affairs

Bound To Him

Santa Daddy's Naughty Baby

ABOUT THE AUTHOR

Cassie Hargrove is an author of all things romance. She is a stay at home mom of three crazy kids. Nine year old autistic twins, and a sassy six year old that 100% takes after her mother.

She lives in a small town with her husband and children, three cats and two dogs. Writing is something she's enjoyed her entire life. It brings an element of calm into the chaos of life.

Newsletter

Printed in Great Britain
by Amazon